Love TANGO

J.M. Jeffries

HARLEQUIN® KIMANI™ ROMANCE

Recycling programs for this product may not exist in your area.

ISBN-13: 978-0-373-86492-8

Love Tango

For questions and comments about the quality of this book please contact us at CustomerService@Harlequin.com.

HARLEQUIN®
www.Harlequin.com

Printed in U.S.A.

Jackie and Miriam have been writing partners for twenty years, though some days it feels like forever. Jackie is a spontaneous writer and Miriam is the planner. Despite such diverse approaches to writing, they have managed to achieve a balance between their unique styles. Jackie is creative, passionate and dedicated. Miriam is focused, thoughtful and detail-oriented. Jackie loves dogs and thinks she doesn't have enough of them. Miriam loves cats, though currently, she is catless. Between the two of them, they work hard to bring their stories to life.

Books by J.M. Jeffries

Harlequin Kimani Romance

Virgin Seductress
My Only Christmas Wish
California Christmas Dreams
Love Takes All
Love's Wager
Bet on My Heart
Drawing Hearts
Blossoms of Love
Love Tango

To all our loyal readers: thank you for trusting us and allowing us to tell the stories of our hearts.

Acknowledgments

To the entire Harlequin Kimani Romance team, thank you for all of your hard work, dedication and patience. You make us look good.

Chapter 1

Roxanne Deveraux sat at her dining room table, genealogy charts spread out around her. The front door to her house slammed. No one slammed a door like her sister, Portia.

Portia stormed into the dining room, thumped her purse down on the table and glared at her sister. She dropped a pile of scripts down on the table. "Here's your weekly pile of scripts from Mom and Dad."

"What's wrong?" Roxanne asked in a mild voice designed to calm her sister. For almost the first half of her life, she had been the peacemaker, the problem solver in a family that thrived on chaos.

"I'll tell you in a minute. Did you know you're trending?" Portia asked, as she pulled out her iPad, woke it up and scrolled through the screens. "In fact, you have been for the last three days."

"I really haven't done anything."

"You play a corpse for five minutes on *Bayside PD* and people take notice. After all, it's the number one cop show."

"I was alive for thirty seconds before I was a corpse." Acting was now her creative hobby and she used her gigs to get celebrity clients for her genealogy business and keep her SAG membership active. "Even a corpse on a number one show gets paid and I get to look at hot actors."

"Mom and Dad weren't impressed." Portia took several deep breaths, as though willing herself to calm down. The anger in her dark brown eyes slowly faded and her breathing evened out.

"I do it just to irritate them." Roxanne stood and neatly gathered up the charts and placed them in a folder next to her laptop.

"Mom says it's a waste of your talent." She gestured at the pile of scripts. "Plus even a bit part is going to give you money that isn't going into their pockets, which is also a point of contention."

"No, it's not. I get exactly what I need out of it." Even though she hadn't talked to her parents in years, they still felt the need to meddle in her life.

Portia's phone chimed and she rummaged in her purse for her phone and turned it completely off.

For two women from the same parents they were as dissimilar as two sisters could be. They resembled each other in their facial structure, high cheekbones, large brown eyes and elegant lips.

Roxanne stood five foot ten in her stocking feet, slim and trim from all the jogging and yoga she did. Portia, at twenty-two, was six years younger, five inches shorter, curvier in the bosom and hips and in some ways more volatile. She was into kickboxing and tae kwon do. While Roxanne's hair was cut into a fashionable shape and left in its natural curly state, Portia had gone for a straightened hairdo, cut into a stylish bob in a Naomi Campbell way. Portia's tawny skin tone and amber eyes were slightly darker than Roxanne's.

Roxanne liked to dress in casual clothing, though today she wore a black pencil skirt with a scarlet leather jacket belted around the waist, black kitten heel shoes and a gold locket nestled against her throat. Portia, who was more fashion conscious and usually wore clothes more cutting-edge in the latest trend, had chosen an ivory pants suit with a short black jacket and a colorful Hermès scarf. A platinum necklace in the shape of a panther with emerald eyes winked against the darkness of her jacket.

"Going back to why you're angry at Mom and Dad."

Portia sighed. "Among many things, they want me to convince you to let them be your agents again. Even the residuals from your old sitcom still bring in a lot of money and they want to capitalize on it."

While the residuals were okay, each year brought a little less since the show wasn't always on the schedule as it became dated and secondary networks had more choices. She was still dependent on her parents sending her the money since it went to them first. She couldn't always depend on them paying out in a timely manner.

Portia gestured at the pile of scripts and picked up the one on top. "I'm supposed to talk you into this movie."

"I was in a movie last year."

"You played a salesgirl. You were on screen for exactly four and half minutes."

"I enjoyed that role, small as it was."

Portia issued another sigh. She picked up the script and held it out to Roxanne. "If you accept this role, their commission will pay the balance of Dad's past-due taxes. You've always been the big moneymaker in the family. Me, I'm just a minor actress who does commercials and voice-overs. Plus the positive media they'd get from having you involved with one of their projects—especially since things have gone downhill since your emancipation—would go a long way into reviving their business reputation."

"I'm not interested in helping him pay off his back taxes. Dad's IRS problem isn't our fault," Roxanne said. "He did it on his own. If he'd filed properly and claimed all the income he was supposed to claim, he wouldn't be in this fix." Instead of trying to hide the fact that he'd borrowed heavily from her trust fund for reasons he'd never totally explained.

"His scheduled payments are going to last at least another two years. Failure to make any of his payments on time could land him in jail. I'm counting the days until I can stop working and maybe get in to UC Davis." Portia had always been into animal rescue and her dream was to be a veterinarian. In her spare time she volunteered at the Los Angeles Zoo.

"But..." Roxanne coaxed. She'd offered to pay for her schooling, but Portia turned her down time after time because their parents already exploited Roxanne for money and Portia felt accepting money from her sister would make her just like them.

"They're pressuring me to sign another two-year contract with them. I feel guilty because I don't want to stay in this business and yet—" she paused, the conflict she was feeling showing on her face "—even I can't argue with the money. I have almost enough put away for school."

"You always were the nice daughter." Roxanne gave her sister a kiss on the cheek.

Portia rubbed her forehead and Roxanne hoped one of her migraines wasn't about to start.

Portia frowned. "I'd rather be like you—the smart, stealthy daughter who got away."

Roxanne's parents had never forgiven her for emancipating herself when she was sixteen and all but walking away from the business. After eleven years on a popular family sitcom, she hadn't wanted to be a full-time actress anymore. The industry had become more and more obsessed with an actress's physical appearance and less appreciative of a woman's talent, and Roxanne was tired of fitting into someone else's mold. With her grandmother's encouragement, she'd won an early admittance to Berkeley and eventually earned a degree in history at the age of twenty and her parents hadn't spoken to her since.

Roxanne, who'd always been interested in genealogy, had taken her hobby and turned it into a small business that she'd been trying to expand into something more the past couple years. She used her own colorful ancestry, which had turned out to be filled with swindlers and con artists, as part of her sales pitch to her clients to show them what could be found.

"You look really nice." Portia motioned for Roxanne to turn around, studying her clothes. "You should have worn those stilettos instead of the shoes you're wearing. I know they add inches to your height you don't want, but they make your legs look really long and sexy and every man in the restaurant will be watching you."

She didn't want every man in the restaurant watching her—especially when she might fall on her face walking in stilettos. She wouldn't consider herself the most coordinated.

Portia reached behind her neck and unfastened her panther necklace. "Take off that locket and wear this instead."

"Where did you get that?" Roxanne hadn't seen the necklace before.

"Mom bought it and then decided she didn't like it and gave it to me. It's really more your style than mine anyway, but I like it."

"Like Nancy is going to care what I'm wearing."

Roxanne had met Nancy several years ago when Roxanne had a small part on a sitcom Nancy's husband, Mike, produced. Nancy had been on the set and curious about an ancestry chart Roxanne had done for another member of the cast. Curious about her own ancestry, Nancy hired Roxanne to investigate and they'd become friends. Portia, who occasionally helped with the searches, had formed her own friendship with the older woman. Roxanne fastened the heavy platinum necklace around her neck and glanced at herself in the mirror over the sideboard. She'd worn her hair up in a French twist. The necklace added just that last bit of style she knew she needed to emphasize her long, slender neck. Leave it to Portia to recognize exactly what would complete an outfit.

"Nancy is all about appearances and she expects you to show up looking classy," Portia said, opening the front door and gesturing toward the car. "Let's go, you know how Nancy hates waiting."

"Nancy," Roxanne said, surprised. "I hope we're not late." Ever since Nancy's phone call asking to meet for lunch at her favorite restaurant, Believe, Roxanne had been curious.

Nancy Bertram was a tiny woman, barely five feet tall with an even tinier waist. Roxanne found it hard to believe her petite body had birthed two lusty boys and one girl. But more than that, Roxanne had always envied Nancy's unerring sense of fashion, from the peach Louboutins on her feet to the matching Chanel suit and tiny gold starburst pin on the collar.

The hostess seated them in a comfortable booth in the back of the restaurant and handed them menus.

"What's going on?" Roxanne asked. "You seemed urgent to see me."

Nancy grinned. "My husband sent me to ask if you'd

like to be on *Celebrity Dance*." Her husband produced a number of shows, all of them dramas except for *Celebrity Dance*.

Roxanne's stomach dropped to the floor. Dancing? On television? This wasn't acting, this was a coordination test—one she was sure to fail.

"What? I mean why?" *Celebrity Dance* had only been on television for a year, but was already popular, challenging *Dancing with the Stars* for top ratings. Roxanne had a hard time seeing herself on the show. She wasn't very graceful and didn't know how to dance.

Nancy whipped out her iPad and swiped across the screen. She held it out to Roxanne. "Have you read any of the comments about your small role in *Bayside PD* from the last episode?"

"I never read those comments. The only thing I read is to make sure my name is spelled correctly on my paycheck."

Nancy took her iPad back. "In the few minutes your character was on scene, you created your own following. People bonded with your character and spent the rest of the show wondering who killed you and why."

"A lot of advertising featured me in it. Maybe the audience was just curious."

"*Bayside PD* has been solidly placed this year and ratings have been steadily growing. Something about this episode just piqued a lot of interest in your character." Nancy shook her head, her elegant blond bob swishing back and forth and settling back into style without one hair out of place.

"I told her she was trending," Portia put in.

Nancy smiled at Roxanne. "Don't you miss being the center of attention?"

Did she miss the attention? Not really. "What I miss is getting to pretend to be someone else for a while. It's like being a superhero with your mother's towel wrapped around your neck to make a cape, but the next morning you're back to being you."

Nancy laughed and Portia shook her head. "Not that we ever did that?"

"You didn't!" Roxanne said in mock dismay at her sister.

Nancy waved her hands as though settling a cape around her shoulders. "My mother had a gold silk capelet that was the perfect length when I was five. Though I don't think she ever forgave me when I jumped in the pool wearing it because I was pretending to save the dog."

Roxanne and Portia joined her in laughter.

"But that's all it is, playtime." Roxanne and Portia's mother had not been thrilled to discover her expensive towels being used as superhero capes.

"Which brings us back to why I wanted to have lunch with you." Nancy put her iPad back in its jacket. "You know Mike and his friend Nicholas Torres developed *Celebrity Dance*. Nick had this idea to let the audience choose the next contestants for the summer season. And your name came up in the top three. Apparently, you have the most loyal following despite the fact you haven't done more than a few roles here and there since *Family Tree* was canceled. And I've been tasked to get you to agree to be on the show."

"I don't know..." she countered.

"You mean you don't want to do it?" Nancy said, her voice clipped.

The last thing she wanted was to alienate Nancy. The woman had been one of her first clients and was well connected. She was also very protective of her husband's business interests. Nancy might like Roxanne a lot, but clearly she wouldn't take kindly to anyone letting her husband down. Roxanne couldn't blame her. Hollywood was full of backstabbers. Loyalty was something rare and valuable—even among spouses.

Roxanne owed Nancy for helping her with her fledgling genealogy business.

"I like to dance," Roxanne said, hesitantly. "I'm not good at it, but I do enjoy a rousing polka."

"Perfect." Nancy pulled out her phone. "After lunch we'll head over to Mike's office. He would like to meet you."

"I should take my sister home first."

"Nonsense. Bring her along. Mike won't mind. I'll keep her occupied."

Portia clapped her hands. "This sounds like fun!"

Fun. Right. Roxanne had some reservations. Who would they pair her with? And what in the hell had she gotten herself into?

Mike Bertram's office was large enough to hold a dozen people. A large picture window overlooked the street. Bookshelves lined one whole wall and were stuffed with scripts and books. A huge black glass desk sat across a corner and Mike stood in front of it with a tall, slim man. Mike was shorter than Roxanne, slightly paunchy, but with a friendly face and kind eyes. He wore an expensive black suit, snow-white shirt and red tie.

"Roxanne, thank you for coming," Mike said holding out his hand. His head barely came to her shoulder and his handshake was soft. "Let me introduce you to my business partner, Nicholas Torres."

She shook Mike's hand and turned to Nicholas Torres. She caught her breath. Nicholas Torres was more handsome in person than on TV. He not only produced the show, but was the lead dancer for *Celebrity Dance.* Nicholas was tall and lithe, but with a muscular catlike grace as he walked to her and shook her hand. His hand was warm and strong. His skin was a pleasing light cinnamon tone and his eyes were gray-brown flecked with green. He was dressed more casually in dark blue pants, a steel-gray shirt at the neck, no jacket or tie. His hair was cut tight to his head and he wore a diamond stud in one ear. She especially liked the fact that he towered over her by several inches—something most men didn't do.

His handshake was pleasantly firm without being crushing. "I'm pleased to meet you, Miss Deveraux."

Something about him made her insides go all hot and gooey. Roxanne grinned at him. "Please, call me Roxanne," she said, her voice sounding a little breathy. Hmm… It had been a long time since she had been so immediately taken by a man. She was surprised.

He smiled, revealing straight white teeth. "I'm Nick. Shall we sit down?" He gestured at a grouping of chairs in a corner surrounding a coffee table with a glass top. A tray with coffee cups and a pot rested on one end. "I understand you started a business doing genealogy."

Roxanne began, after taking a long, slow breath to calm herself, "It's still in its infancy stage. Most of my clients have come from the shows I've worked on. Genealogy is one of the fastest growing hobbies in America." She laughed. "Did I just sound like an infomercial?"

Nick grinned at her. "You sounded like you're passionate about genealogy."

"I am." Roxanne glanced at Nancy who took a seat at the bar with Portia next to her.

"Mike," Roxanne said, "didn't you find it exciting to know Nancy is descended from the Sun King, Louis XIV, through one of his mistresses?"

"I didn't need to know that to recognize she was royalty." Mike blushed a little after a quick glance at his wife. "My own ancestry was a bit of a surprise. Who knew I came from a long line of entertainers? I don't have a talented bone in my body. And when you showed me that one of my ancestors was sponsored by King Charles II of England, I was surprised. And even more surprised to find out he liked playing female roles." Mike gave a short, self-deprecating laugh.

"That was a lucky find. Women weren't allowed on the stage at that time," Roxanne said. "They weren't allowed to do much besides produce more little humans. So nice to know we've come such a long way."

Nick Torres had a deep, pleasant laugh. "I'll admit, I'm a little curious myself about my ancestors."

"It's like a trail. Finding all the landmarks is fun and

exciting and people learn about history in a very personal way because it grounds us to our past and makes everything real. I remember in high school how bored I was by historical facts that had little context for me. But finding out about my ancestors made history come to life."

Mike beamed, obviously proud of his ancestry. "What happens when you don't find anything?"

"The internet is pretty extensive when it comes to ancestry searches," Roxanne explained, "but sometimes records are lost or haven't been digitized yet, and that's when the real work starts. But there's always a trail of some sort no matter how tiny. It could be something as simple as a marriage certificate or a birth certificate. My great-grandfather's WWII service records were lost in a fire, but I found his draft card. That wasn't much, but it did give me a context to work from and I discovered my great-grandfather was stationed at Pearl Harbor the day Japan bombed it and I was able to find the son of one of the men he served with, who actually remembered my great-grandfather." That had been a happy accident that had added another piece to the jigsaw puzzle of her family history.

"Sounds like fun," Nick said, "but what we really wanted to talk to you about is being on *Celebrity Dance*."

Roxanne smiled at him. "I love to dance, but I'm a little on the klutzy side." She didn't add she was five foot ten. They could see that for themselves.

She also didn't add that she really didn't want to do the show but felt obligated to do it. She only hoped she still had her dignity intact when it was over.

"You've been turning up in a lot of bit parts lately."

"Just keeping my hand in the business."

"Are you thinking about making a full-blown return?"

"I don't want to do a weekly show anymore or movies. I'm really happy just doing little bit parts here and there. And being a corpse works just fine." She'd thought she'd hated acting, but after a few years and a lot of thought she realized she enjoyed acting on a limited basis. Her parents' manipulation of her had been what she'd really despised.

"But being a corpse isn't much of a challenge," Nick said.

"Are you making fun of me?" She felt a stab of disappointment that he would judge her without knowing anything about her.

He looked startled. "No. I'm sorry. I didn't mean to..."

She said defensively, "You try holding your breath and looking dead at the same time for a minute or two and not turn blue." She wondered if she could specialize in corpse acting. Was there such a thing? She liked the short jobs. In their own way, they were fun. Those jobs weren't a challenge. She wasn't in *Death of a Salesman.* Nick and Mike laughed. She glanced at Nancy and Portia who had zoned out and were bonding over their shoes.

"Your name has been showing up in a lot of places lately," Mike said.

"Which I don't understand." Roxanne gave a little shrug.

"So, you're not a fan of social media."

"I'm more connected to the past."

"Does your business pay well?" Nick asked.

"It does when I have celebrity clients. You'd be surprised how many actors and actresses are disappointed when they find out Shakespeare isn't in their family tree."

Nick grinned at her and the beauty of his smile made her blood race. She imagined herself in his arms and heat rose in her. "I can guarantee he's not in my family tree?"

"Don't be so certain," Roxanne cautioned, but she wasn't sure if she was speaking to him or herself.

"What do you mean?"

"There's been some controversy that Shakespeare had a longtime black mistress. And the fact that he wrote *Othello* does give us some clues into his social group."

He looked so surprised, she laughed.

"If I agree to go on *Celebrity Dance*, who are you going to partner me with. LeBron James?"

"How about me?" Nick asked. He stood and pulled her to her feet. With her hands in his she stared into his eyes and tried not to focus on his very kissable mouth so close to hers.

"Well, I am enjoying looking up at you." The top of her head was just even with his nose. His eyes held a sparkle that let her know he was attracted to her, too.

He took her in his arms and started to draw her into a simple waltz. She smiled at him and immediately stepped on his foot and a second later tripped on an uneven spot on the rug.

"Sorry," she said. "Sorry." Portia and Nancy clapped.

Roxanne gave her sister her best stare-down which made Portia burst into laughter.

"That's okay," he said with a grin. "I like to know I have my work cut out for me."

Mike stood and held out his hand to Roxanne. "My legal department will be getting in touch with your agent."

"Trudy Mendoza handles my legal affairs." Everyone knew Trudy. She was one of the best entertainment lawyers in the industry. She'd handled Roxanne's emancipation and had become a friend along the way.

"That is one tall woman," Mike said.

"I like tall women," Nick said. And boy, did she have legs. A little fantasy played out in his mind with her legs wrapped around him. Heat spiraled through him and he stood up and walked to the window. He saw the women exit to the street and make their way to the parking structure.

"You two are going to look good together," Mike continued. "But her parents are a piece of work."

Nick had only been back in Los Angeles for a couple years and wasn't up on all the current gossip. He'd had his own controversies in New York. He'd been involved with a Broadway star. Things had ended badly. She'd stalked him all the way to Los Angeles and the situation didn't end until she'd been checked into a very nice mental facility. The movers and shakers on Broadway had been furious with him, because he'd put a guaranteed moneymaking legend out of business during the run of a very productive play. Nick had been lucky to escape to Los Angeles even though his reputation in New York was in tatters. Nobody liked whistle-blowers even when they were in the right.

Mike nodded. "Her parents wanted her to do this movie to get around child labor laws. They encouraged her to apply for emancipation. She did, was emancipated and refused to do the movie saying it made her uncomfortable. Before the emancipation came through, they tried to force her, but she had the brains to hire Trudy Mendoza…"

"I remember Trudy Mendoza. She's the shark all the great whites sharks are afraid of."

"She discovered some financial misconduct and before her parents knew anything, she was out from under their thumb. The news was she was able to get her high school diploma early. She ended up at Berkeley."

Nick vaguely remembered the gossip, but hadn't paid that much attention. The parents didn't stay down long, because they specialized in managing child actors. Plus they had two more of their own biological children to exploit, not as talented as Roxanne who had been the big moneymaker, but still bankable.

Nick said, "You think when her parents hear about her being on the show that they are going to be trouble?"

"Nancy tells me," Mike said, "they have been trying to get back into her good graces for years. She's still a moneymaker if she wants to be. The public loves her."

Nick could see why. She was just the kind of person he liked. Besides being beautiful, she was smart and funny.

"We have a nice lineup for the second season of

Celebrity Dance," Nick said. He liked diversity. Roxanne Deveraux would add just the right kind of spunk and sass that he liked. She could laugh at herself. That LeBron James line was funny. And that look of panic in her eyes when he told her he wanted her as his partner had been priceless.

"She'll work out," Nick continued, suddenly anxious to get her to her first practice. Already he was planning their first dance. They always started with a waltz because it was simple. She would be elegant in burgundy silk with her hair up, showing off her long neck. He'd wear a white tuxedo and matching top hat. He found himself swaying as he imagined their waltz.

"Nick. Nick. Nick. Where are you, Nick? Come back to me."

Nick came back with a start. "Sorry, my mind was wandering."

"I could tell," Mike said with a wry tone. "I need to call the lawyers and get them working on her contract. You need to get back to the studio. The publicist is sending me urgent SOSs. He's been receiving calls all morning regarding the guests for our summer season and when we'll release the list."

Nick had to laugh. "I'll go help him field the calls."

In the car, Roxanne handed her keys to her sister, climbed onto the passenger seat and leaned her head back as Portia cleanly navigated out of the parking structure and onto the street heading for the freeway.

"Thank you for the emotional support at that meeting."

"You were fabulous."

"You never did tell me what Mom and Dad want you to do?" Roxanne said, suppressing a yawn.

Portia drove up the entry ramp and merged into traffic heading back to Pacific Palisades. "You know who Javier Gomez is, don't you?"

"I have absolutely no idea."

"You probably know him as El Gomez. He got his start in Mexico composing *narco corridos* and managed to make the transition to the LA music scene."

Roxanne stared at her sister. "What are *narco corridos*?" She had no idea who El Gomez was.

"Mexican ballads that glorify the drug trade and the crime lords in Mexico. Mom and Dad want me to date him."

Roxanne sat up straight. "Are your parents insane?"

"They are your parents, too." Portia said with a laugh.

"Only through the sharing of DNA. What…what… huh…what… The words just won't come."

"He's edgy and trending. He has three million Twitter followers and another five million on Instagram. And he's a kid. I'm twenty-two years old and he's eighteen. He still acts like he's the hot man on the high school campus. He struts. All he has to do is point his finger at whichever groupie is following him around at that moment and she falls at his feet." Portia shuddered.

Roxanne opened the browser on her phone and did a quick search. A photo appeared of a good-looking teenager in a slick Latin sort of way. "He has a face tattoo."

"And a tongue stud, ear plugs and a nose ring. He has more jewelry on his body than I have in my jewelry box. And he's four inches shorter than me and I'm not tall to begin with."

Roxanne scrolled through the photos and articles. "What do Mom and Dad think your dating this…this… man-child is going to accomplish?"

"The Latin market is the fastest-growing market on TV—discretionary income and, well, just about everything. They think it would be good for my career. They want me to be the first black actress on a telenovela because I speak Spanish so well."

"I told you to take German in high school," Roxanne said. Portia had been surprisingly good at languages and picked up Spanish in no time. "I repeat—they are insane." And greedy. "What did you tell them?"

"Words wouldn't come out of my mouth. I just got up and left."

"Is our brother on board with this?"

"He hasn't objected. It was originally Dad's idea, and if I wasn't driving, I'd add air quotes to 'they're all bros now.' I'd feel like Esther the molester."

Roxanne continued to read. "Do Mom and Dad realize his uncle is Manuel Gomez? He runs the second-largest drug cartel in Mexico." Her parents may have been the most difficult people on the face of the earth, but they didn't condone drugs. For that, Roxanne had to admire them. She started laughing.

"What's so funny?"

"I just went to my future place and had this image of your wedding. His side of the church, your side of the church and the DEA in the middle."

"Stop trying to make me laugh. Right now, I'm picturing my bridesmaids in jailhouse orange."

"Since I'll be your maid of honor, can I wear horizontal stripes and carry a bouquet that could double as a prison weapon?"

"Stop," Portia begged. "I'm going to run off the road trying not to laugh."

"We can serve prison-gourmet food of chicken nuggets and peanut-butter-and-jelly sandwiches," Roxanne continued, the image in her mind growing more detailed. "And sit on hard benches and bang our plastic utensils on the table."

"We're done," Portia said. "My stomach hurts from trying not to laugh. But the reality is…he scares me. And what happens if being around him makes me a target, too?"

Roxanne sobered. The more she read about El Gomez the more he frightened her, too. "They can't force you to date him. You're a grown woman. If you want to walk away, I can help. I have money and I can protect you."

"I'm fine," Portia said. "I like doing the commercials and voice-overs. And I'll deal with Mom and Dad."

Roxanne didn't say anything to her sister—Portia needed her dream of escape—but their parents wouldn't let her go easily. She might be only twenty-two but as the middle child, she was the family peacemaker with their parents using her as a buffer even between themselves. She didn't like the chaos or drama that dominated their parents' lives and did her best to soothe difficult moments, to keep things running smoothly.

They would find a way to keep her trapped. Roxanne pondered what she could do to help, but nothing came to her. Sometimes she felt sad that she'd extricated herself from the chaos that was the Deveraux family and left her brother and sister behind. When she'd been sixteen, she'd been more worried about herself and anxious to get away. She never thought about how her parents would exploit Portia and Tristan. And now, with her parents all of a sudden encouraging their kids to run with people with hardcore criminal ties, she knew she had to do something. She just didn't know what. She would again offer to pay Portia's college tuition or cosign for a loan, and maybe this time she'd accept.

Chapter 2

"I was surprised when you called me." Surprised but pleased. Roxanne sat down at the sidewalk table across from Nicholas Torres.

The restaurant bordered Santa Monica Boulevard. Nicholas Torres had chosen an outside table to enjoy the pleasantly warm afternoon and watch the young people on spring break crossing the Pacific Coast Highway and making their way to the beach. In the distance she could hear the faintest roar of the waves and smell the tangy salt air. She loved living by the ocean.

"You looked a little uneasy yesterday," Nick said, "and Nancy told me you're concerned about being clumsy."

A waitress handed her a menu and she asked for a glass of water.

"*Uneasy* was not the word I would use."

Nick grinned at her. "What word would you use?"

"How about apprehensive, troubled or edgy? Or better yet, let's try the phrase *full-blown panic*." The waitress brought her water and she ordered a Greek salad with extra Kalamata olives.

"You seem very graceful to me," Nick added.

"First of all, I wear flat shoes, walk slowly and concentrate on what I'm doing."

"Dancing is the same thing."

"At a much quicker pace. And then I have to throw in breathing and trying to look comfortable. I've seen some of the dresses you've put your contestants in. You know the scene with Fred Astaire and Ginger Rogers where she's wearing this white dress with feathers. That is the most beautiful, seductive dance scene in the whole of movie history and all he could talk about was the feathers that kept flying into his mouth. I'm not Ginger Rogers. I'm the feathers—all over the place and in your mouth." Oops, that was very suggestive. Heat spread across her cheeks. "Let me rephrase that…"

Nick just laughed. "Oh, no. You are funny."

"Yeah I'm hilarious," she said.

"You'll do fine," Nick said. "Again, the best dancer doesn't always win. When you strip away all the glitter and sweat, it's really a popularity contest. The person who wins is the one that connects with the audience the most. You've got that in the bag."

"Then why do we have to dance? Why can't we just be us and pose prettily?"

"Do you not want be on *Celebrity Dance*?"

She paused for a second thinking. "I'm going to be

on your show. I'm going to practice my little heart out. I just don't want you to be disappointed in me when I don't measure up to your standards." She had spent last night watching reruns on YouTube. His grace and talent took her breath away. She'd seen him dance on the show and watched clips of him on Broadway. That man could move like a cloud. Did he have any idea how sexy he looked? How strong and masculine. Oh, he gave her tingles in all the right places.

The waitress brought her salad and placed a thick steak sandwich in front of Nick. Their conversation paused while they took a few bites. "People who don't try disappoint me." He popped a french fry into his mouth and chewed. "I come from a big family. I have four brothers and two sisters and we're all competitive. We all want to win. We all want to be king of the hill." He smiled as though the nostalgic memories were pleasant.

Her own family was more about backstabbing, which made her sad. Weren't parents supposed to love and protect their children? Hers had exploited her, and their selfish needs had superseded hers and her siblings'. "I haven't done anything truly competitive in a few years, and I'm not afraid of anything, but there's a reason my parents didn't name me Grace."

Nick grinned. "I'm happy my mother didn't let my dad name me Heriberto and my twin brother Mattero like he wanted to."

Roxanne started to laugh. She was enjoying her lunch with Nick. He was an entertaining man and from some of the looks she was getting from women at other tables, they were just a touch envious she was the one having lunch with the most handsome man in the whole restaurant.

"What happens next?" Roxanne asked. Her salad was delicious and the company was delightful. She felt herself relaxing.

"The official announcement of the next season's contestants will be on *The Morning Show with Daniel Torres* next Monday and then later on *Entertainment Tonight* and *The Insider*, but before then, we'll be doing short little interviews that will go up on the show's website immediately after the announcement. I want to set up a time for you to come in for an interview. My assistant will call you later today with your schedule. We'll start with hair, makeup and head shots, then do the interview. Next week after the announcement we're filming a commercial. So you'll need an appointment with the wardrobe department and then you and I will practice a quick dance move for the teaser trailer. Nothing elaborate, just something easy to showcase you."

"I get to practice my dance moves." She flung out her hand trying to quell the nervous fluttering in her stomach and tipped over a glass of water that ended up half in her salad and the rest quickly spreading across the table and dripping down to Nick's pants. "I'm sorry." She sprang up.

The waitress hurried over with napkins and started sopping up the mess.

"I should have just settled for jazz hands," Roxanne said, chagrined at making such a mess. She was never at her best with men and the idea of dancing on TV in front of millions of people was making her more clumsy than normal.

He laughed. "I used to work in a restaurant and this is not the worst thing that has happened to me." He took a pile of napkins and helped the waitress mop up the water. "We're outside in southern California, my clothes will dry."

Heat flooded her face. "I'm so embarrassed."

"Don't cry over spilled water," he said.

The waitress wiped up the last bit of water and picked up the drenched salad. She grinned at Roxanne. "I can remake your salad but, honey, you look like you could use a piece of chocolate-silk cream pie instead."

"No, thank you and I'm done with the salad. I'm going to have to fit in a tight dress."

"Bring her a piece of pie," Nick said, his eyes alight with amusement. "Trust me, you'll work it off starting tomorrow."

Nick found himself chuckling in the car as he drove back to the studio. He hadn't had so much fun with a woman in a long time. He tended to keep things on a light note with the women he normally dated after the bad experience with the stalker had left him shaken.

Roxanne was full of surprises. She had more determination than dance talent, but he could work with that. He wouldn't be able to turn her into a swan, but he could turn her into a competent dancer. Her personality would do the rest. He just had a feeling the audience was going to love her.

Once at the studio, he found himself walking into

his brother's office instead of heading farther down the hall to his own.

Daniel was hunched over his laptop, frowning. He looked up and his face transformed into a smile.

"What cha doin', bro?" Nick said. He flopped into a chair.

Daniel grinned. "Greer wants to design a cake that looks like a parade float and actually moves."

"If anyone can create that, she can. I have total confidence in her." Greer Courtland was Daniel's soon-to-be bride. She also designed parade floats for the Rose Parade. Daniel had been impressed by her talent and fallen in love with her while filming segments of the progress of his Rose Parade float. They were planning a January wedding because Greer wouldn't be able to get away until after October.

"I just want to get married," Daniel said. "I just want her to be mine forever, so everyone can see. All these details are making me crazy. I've spent years looking for her. I never have to date again. I have the woman of my dreams. I just want to get married."

Nick held up his hands. "Whoa, there. What brought this on?"

Daniel scrubbed his face with his hands. "I'm ready to get on with the next phase of my life." Daniel wasn't the most patient man in the world. He could fake patience well, but underneath he would seethe. "Okay. I got that off my chest and can get on with my day. But that needed to be said."

"You need to tell Greer."

"I'm good now. I am willing to have the wedding

of her dreams because it's more important to make her happy. Dad sat down and gave me the 'now that you're getting married' speech. His talk boiled down to his 'happy wife, happy life' metaphor."

"That must have been uncomfortable."

"It was more uncomfortable than the sex talk."

"Yeah, he just gave us a condom and hoped for the best." Nick remembered the talk clearly. He and Daniel had been fifteen and they'd received only one warning from their mother. There would be no Torres baby-daddies, she'd told them. And like their other brothers, they listened.

"I want to grab Greer and head to Vegas like Mom and Dad did."

"And disappoint Nina," Nick said. Their sister was the planner in the family. With Greer and her sisters busy with the floats they was currently building, she'd asked Nina to help with the wedding plans.

Daniel rubbed her temple.

"Good luck, bro," Nick said cheerfully. "I'll leave you to it."

He closed the door on Daniel's groan and headed to his office.

The morning of the announcement, Roxanne was up and out the door by 4:00 a.m. racing for the studio to have her hair and makeup done before the big announcement on Daniel Torres's show. She grabbed her laptop and the file of her current client so she could work during the lulls. She couldn't afford to waste one minute.

The drive from Pacific Palisades to the studio went

more smoothly than normal. No accidents jammed the freeway and traffic was unusually light. She walked into the studio still yawning, a huge cup of coffee in one hand. She never skipped her morning coffee.

After her hair and makeup were finished, she joined the other contestants on the set. Nick reached for her hand and pulled her out slightly ahead of the others.

"We're live in five," the director held up fingers. As each one went down, he silently mouthed the number.

"This is Daniel Torres. Welcome back to *The Morning Show with Daniel Torres*. This morning we have the announcement of the contestants for *Celebrity Dance* season two, starting May 22. I want to welcome everyone."

Daniel stood in the center of the set. He backed away and the camera panned across Roxanne and Nick, down the row of people. She knew three of the contestants already, the rest she had never met. Nick chose a broad spectrum of people. A former astronaut, a football player, a Broadway star, the head of a Fortune 500 company, a politician, along with two actresses, herself and two men she'd never heard of. She tried to memorize the names, but everything happened so fast.

Daniel approached her. "Roxanne Deveraux," he announced her name. "Partnering with Nicholas Torres. You have a strong lineup, Nick, for the coming season."

Nick smiled. "I give a lot of thought to who I think will do well. I look for people who are entertaining, fun and enthusiastic." He stepped to the side and held out a hand. "Like Roxanne here." He twirled her around.

Roxanne tried to stay upright, but one ankle collapsed and she stumbled against Nick. Mortified at her clumsiness, she was amazed when Nick caught her and dipped her. She tried not to look surprised at how smoothly he'd turned her almost tumble into what looked like an orchestrated dance move. She had to admire his ability to think so quickly even as she couldn't stop thinking she'd made a big mistake.

Stilettos just weren't her thing. Plus the fact she felt like André the Giant next to petite Adela Gardiner who stood five foot three.

Nick pulled her upright. "Don't worry, I can work with this."

She smiled for the camera and Daniel moved down to introduce the rest of the contestants. Each one did a small dance step almost flawlessly and Roxanne tried to keep her spirits from sinking. Even the football player was perfect. When Daniel said something, the football player grinned and said he'd taken ballet lessons in high school so he knew where to put his feet.

Roxanne was even more embarrassed. She tried to slide back into the shadows, but Nick kept a tight grip on her hand refusing to let her hide. She kept a grip on her emotions, refusing to think about how she was going to be humiliated. She couldn't back out now, she'd committed and Nancy had faith in her.

Daniel finished introducing everyone and he stepped in front of the camera. "There you have it, Los Angeles. The cast of the summer season of *Celebrity Dance*."

Everyone smiled. Nick whispered to Roxanne, "Stop being embarrassed. You just gave us a leg up in the competition."

"I almost broke your foot," she whispered back.

"You made us the underdog and you know everyone loves an underdog. So smile and look like you're ready to grab the world."

She widened her smile and tried to look like she wasn't cringing inside. She could do this. She was the little train that could.

The rehearsal room was large with walls lined in mirrors.

Roxanne sat on a bench looking tired. "The waltz is so beautiful. How can it be so deadly, so lethal?" She unbuckled her shoes and rubbed her instep.

Nick knelt down in front of her and took one foot. He could feel the cramp in her instep. Slowly, he massaged the tight muscle, marveling at how soft her skin was. "Your muscles will loosen up. It's all about muscle memory."

She sighed. "My body is hoping for amnesia. I have sore muscles I didn't know I had."

Nick laughed. "You're going to be fine." For the past four hours he'd guided her through the steps over and over, adding little routines that changed the waltz and made it more interesting in his opinion. And holding Roxanne in his arms had sent a thousand different signals to his brain. Her scent, her touch, her nearness almost made him breathless and all he knew was that he didn't want to let her go.

"This is our first rehearsal and I fell four times."

Nick continued massaging her instep. "You're getting it out of your system."

"I should be dressed in football padding."

Nick laughed again. "This is the first rehearsal. Just relax, we have plenty of time to make this beautiful. Right now, you have to be comfortable with the dance."

Roxanne groaned. "How long did it take you to learn the waltz?"

He wasn't going to tell her it took him maybe ten minutes to figure out the steps and the rhythm. He'd been five years old at the time and had no idea that dance would play a major role in his future life. "No one is judging me. I know what I'm doing."

"How long?" she pressed.

"Fifteen minutes, tops," he said with a grin. He moved to her other foot and slowly massaged the tight muscles. "But I make my living as a dancer."

"I think I'm going to be making my living from a hospital bed."

"Before you head to the hospital, we'll do some more stretching exercises, then you're going home. Ice your feet and calves, then take a nice, hot bath. If you have a Jacuzzi tub, spend some time in it. Then have a glass of wine and eat a lot of protein. Tomorrow we're really going to get into it."

"What were we doing today?" She stared at him incredulously.

"This was just the start, learning the steps, getting into the feel. Tomorrow you'll see Wardrobe for your first fitting and then back here for another four hours of practice."

She blew a strand of hair out of her eyes. "I'm going home and curling up on the floor." She stood and stumbled. "Ow. Ow. My feet hurt, my legs hurt, my skin hurts and my eyelashes hurt."

Nick smiled at her performance as she limped across the floor barefoot. "Walk it off," he said.

She glared at him. "Twenty hours a week in rehearsal, I'm going to be skin and bones when this over."

"You're going to be skin and bones with muscles you didn't even know you had." And considering how good she looked now, the extra muscle tone would make her look even sleeker and sexier.

She groaned again.

He'd had a lot of dance partners, and Roxanne was the most inexperienced he'd ever had. He was going to enjoy the challenge of whipping her into shape. And he was enjoying her. And he was thinking of ways to enjoy her more. Even though he shouldn't be. She made him laugh.

She grabbed her tote and purse from her locker. She looked down at her feet. "My ankles are swollen. My pinky toe doesn't look right. Is it broken?" She pushed her foot toward him.

"It looks a little pinched from being in those shoes you brought. You might want to look for a wider size."

She grumbled. "Tomorrow I'm bringing my slippers."

She slung her tote and purse over her shoulder and headed out the double doors to the parking lot. Nick followed her. From the way she was hobbling, he felt he needed to get her safely to her car.

The parking lot was mostly empty. She limped toward her white Prius and Nick frowned at the huge black Escalade with tinted windows parked next to it.

As she approached her car, the doors to the Escalade opened and a man and woman stepped out.

Roxanne groaned. "No. Not now." She stopped and Nick stood next to her, every muscle tense in response to her moan.

The woman approached. She was tall and slim and dressed for success in a ruby-red pants suit and black blouse. She wore dark glasses, but even from a distance, Nick could see Roxanne was related to her. The man was also tall, with dark curly hair threaded with gray. He was a little more casual in designer jeans and a white button-down shirt.

"Darling," the woman said as she air-kissed Roxanne.

Roxanne stepped back, avoiding her mother's outstretched arms. "Mother."

"You look…a bit disheveled, dear."

Roxanne glanced around. "What are you doing here?"

From the resemblance, he knew this man was Roxanne's father. He stood back slightly. He removed his dark glasses and studied Roxanne.

Her mother laughed. "Darling, you've become so cynical."

"I wonder why." Roxanne's tone was dry and tart.

Roxanne mother smiled at Nick. "Hello, I'm Hannah Deveraux, Roxanne's mother and this is Eli, her father. And you're Nick Torres. I know all about you." Hannah smiled pleasantly, but Nick knew he was facing a barracuda. A big hungry barracuda.

"What do you want?" Roxanne's voice was strained.

"We haven't spoken much the last few years, but we wanted to congratulate you for being chosen for *Ce-*

lebrity Dance. Such a coup. So much better than playing a corpse."

Hannah's voice was smooth and gracious on the surface, but Nick felt an underlying subtext meant for Roxanne alone.

Hannah turned her dark eyes on Nick. "And you, Nicky, you are so lucky to have Roxanne on your show. She's always wanted to learn how to dance, but her feet never cooperated."

"I prefer Nicholas." Nick ground his teeth together at the passive-aggressive performance by Roxanne's parents. "And Roxanne is going to be great."

Hannah glanced at her daughter's bare feet. "Where are your shoes, sweetie? You shouldn't be walking around barefoot."

"I have to go," Roxanne said, taking a step toward her car. "Nice to see you. Bye."

"But we need to talk," Hannah sidestepped to cut off Roxanne's attempt to escape. "We can put you back on top, sweetie. You'd be on every A-list in town."

"I don't want to be there."

Her mother frowned. "Then why are you doing *Celebrity Dance*?"

Roxanne said nothing, staring her mother down.

Hannah broke the stare down first. "Did you look at the script I sent you? Your father and I own the rights to it. Starring in it could be an opportunity to mend fences. Clear the air."

"No, I haven't read it. Nor do I intend to read it." Roxanne skirted her parents, unlocked her car with the remote in her hand and was in her car before her parents could object.

Nick stood back, half admiring as Roxanne deftly maneuvered her Prius out of its parking space.

Hannah's mouth tightened. "You must pardon my daughter's rudeness."

Nick's eyebrows rose. "She wasn't rude to me at all."

"I hoped she would talk with us," Hannah said with a sad little sigh. "She's so very stubborn. We've only ever wanted the best for our daughter. I don't understand what her problem is. We've done everything for her." She gave Nick a coy, sideways look that contained an invitation to unburden himself in some way.

Nick edged back. He needed to get out of here. Confession wasn't going to be good for their souls and he had a sense they were trying to enlist him.

"I have to get back." He took another step away from them.

"We need you to help us," Hannah continued. "Will you talk to Roxanne for us? Tell her we love her and only have her best interests at heart."

"I don't mean to be rude, but that isn't my job. We're coworkers and that's all. So you have a nice day."

When he glanced back, Hannah and Eli stood in the middle of the parking lot. Hannah's gestures were sharp and angry. Eli's gestures matched hers. Nick wondered what they were arguing about. After a few minutes they climbed back into the black Escalade and peeled out of the parking lot with a squeal of tires and burning rubber.

Once they were gone, Nick pulled his phone out of his pocket and dialed Mike's number. "We need to talk.

I'll be at the office in thirty minutes." He disconnected and walked toward the locker room to get his stuff.

Nick opened the door to Mike's office. His wife, Nancy, sat on the sofa, her legs crossed, hands fluttering as she laughed at whatever Mike had said.

Mike looked up. He sat at his desk, one hand poised over a stack of papers. "How did the first rehearsal go?"

"She stepped on my feet eight hundred times. She tripped over her own feet at least four times. She's a challenge."

"You love a challenge," Nancy said.

"You're right, I do. And she is that." Nick perched on the corner of Mike's desk.

"Last year, you took over an overweight, over-the-hill actress..."

"Ouch," Nick said.

"Those were Mia's words, not mine... And you made her a dance champion and resurrected her career. She's going to be in the next Joss Whedon film playing a superhero."

"Roxanne," Nancy added, "is young, fit and easy to look at. She's got a lot of personality."

And she was a delight to hold, Nick thought. Her skin was soft and her subtle perfume filled him with desire. "Her lack of grace is not going to be the problem."

"What's going to be the problem?" Mike asked curiously.

"Her parents," Nick said with a sigh. "They were waiting in the parking lot after rehearsal. And I think things could have gotten incredibly nasty." The kind of nasty that could end up in the gossip rags. True or not, the information crippled anyone involved.

Mike rubbed his temple. "I'm glad Roxanne is not contractually obligated to them in any way. That could just be ugly."

"They're her family," Nick said. His own family was so different. They supported each other.

"Family means nothing in this town. It's what's written down on paper that counts."

Nick shook his head. "I still think they are going to be a problem."

"I don't think much is going to stop them from being a problem," Nancy added.

"You've been friends with Roxanne for several years now. What does she say about her parents?"

"Nothing," Nancy replied. "She never talks about them and I don't ask."

"Roxanne is a nice woman and I like her." He liked her a lot. "Her parents might prove a big enough distraction to keep her from doing her best." Roxanne had an honesty about her that appealed to him. She had no illusions about who she was.

Nancy frowned. "Roxanne is too classy to get dragged into a tawdry controversy with her parents. And I don't want to see her hurt."

Mike looked thoughtful. "Controversy can be great publicity, but it's not something I want for my show. I don't want this season to be overshadowed by a mudslinging war between Roxanne and her parents. It's unfair to the other contestants who are actually trying to revive their careers. Plus it creates all kinds of tension on the set."

"Do you honestly think that will happen?" Nick asked, although he knew the answer.

"You know how the paparazzi and gossip rags love that kind of stuff," Mike replied.

Roxanne pulled into her driveway to find Portia's car parked on the street.

"What are you doing here?" Roxanne asked after walking into her home.

Portia stood in the kitchen making a chicken-salad sandwich. She wore her zoo uniform with the faint hint of hay clinging to her. She held a knife and waved it through the air. "Mom and Dad sent me."

Roxanne stopped and stared at her sister. "Speak of the devils, I just ran into them. They were waiting for me outside the rehearsal studio."

Portia patted the top piece of bread into place, cut it and took a bite. She chewed her food for a half minute, swallowed and took a sip of iced tea. "Well, they want to bury the hatchet, extend an olive branch, so to speak. Whatever they can do to bring you back into the fold. I'm supposed to be their ambassador."

Roxanne opened the refrigerator and grabbed a soda. "Why?"

"They're bleeding clients like mad. Mom and Dad are giving them all the runaround while they're trying to sort out their finances. Having the IRS hanging over them every second is messing with their ability to run their business, and even though none of the clients know the details of their tax troubles, Mom and Dad's erratic behavior about the whole situation is not breeding confidence in their ability to handle their clients' affairs because they can't seem to handle their own. And this script they want you to read, they own the rights and it's actually pretty good."

"So why don't they get another actress—a bigger actress? Tons of actresses would kill for a great starring role." Even as the words left her mouth, Roxanne knew the answer.

Portia gave her an exasperated look. "Public relations. Image rebuilding. Think about it. They have a great script. And with the prodigal daughter partnering with them on it—you know how far that would go to rebuild their image. If you trust them, others would, too."

Roxanne knew. The industry was full of sheep. Where one went, often more followed.

Portia sat at the table across from Roxanne. "I just spent the morning brainstorming with them and their plan of attack is to bring you back into the warm embrace of our harmonious family and take advantage of your new fame on *Celebrity Dance*. If they can get you back for this film and show that you have every confidence in them, they would be able to rebuild their client base."

"Ow," Roxanne said. "Whose idea was that?"

"Tristan's."

"Oh, baby brother."

"He desperately wants to be on Broadway, especially since his character is being written out of that medical drama he's on, and the lead in the revival of *Timbuktu* is coming up for audition. Even I know he's perfect for the role."

Roxanne said in a jaundiced tone, "He's going to have to give up drinking, partying and chasing women. That type of behavior is only excused when you reach the top."

Portia nodded as she bit into her sandwich and gave a little sigh. She ate in silence for a few minutes. "Mom and Dad are frantic."

"They're seeing their little empire crumble around them."

Roxanne didn't want to be drawn back into her parents' domain. Until she'd turned sixteen, she'd been under their controlling thumb and spent a lot of days resenting them.

The garage door opened and their grandmother walked into the kitchen carrying a load of grocery bags. "Hello, girls."

Portia jumped up to kiss Donna Deveraux on the cheek. Like Portia, Donna was small and compact with gray hair cut tight to her head and expressive brown eyes. Her voice still held a hint of Southern cadence from her Mississippi childhood. Her eyes lit up at the sight of her granddaughters.

"I wasn't expecting to see you, Portia. Are you staying for dinner?" Donna asked as she set grocery bags on the counter.

"Sure." Portia said. "I was hoping we could have a slumber party tonight."

Roxanne kissed her grandmother on the cheek and set about unpacking the groceries and putting them away.

"We can do that," Donna said.

If not for her grandmother, Roxanne might have gone insane as a child. Donna had cared for her, home-schooled her, acted as guardian when Roxanne was on the set and generally kept her grounded in the real world. Donna had always been around when Roxanne needed her and once she'd graduated college and bought this house, she'd moved her grandmother in with her. She'd set up a modest trust fund that generously supplemented her grandmother's social security because somewhere down through the years, her parents had forgotten to pay her for her services. When Roxanne had found out, she'd been livid.

"Grams," Roxanne said, "What are you cooking tonight?"

Donna grinned at her granddaughters. "Chicken and dumplings, child." She reached into one of the plastic bags. "And a bottle of your favorite pinot grigio."

"Maybe not," Portia said. "I'm being considered as the lead in a series of commercials for some car ads."

Roxanne countered, hating to see her sister deprive herself. The industry was merciless on women who weren't a size two. "One decadent meal isn't going to kill your figure."

Portia looked thoughtful. "I can always spend a little more time working out tomorrow."

Roxanne took the wine bottle and put it in the refrigerator to chill.

"Are we celebrating something?" Portia asked.

"I just felt like doing something special." Donna opened a cabinet and pulled out a large pan. "How did your first rehearsal go?"

"My feet hurt," Roxanne said. "I want to soak my abused toes and everything else in between that and my ears. I stepped on Nick's toes so many times, I'm surprised they aren't broken, and tripped over my own feet. I lost count after five."

"That bad, was it?" Donna said.

"And that wasn't the worst part. Mommy and Daddy showed up."

Donna's eyes narrowed. "And they wanted what?"

"They want me to read that script Portia brought a couple weeks ago." Roxanne sat down at the table and cupped her chin in the palm of one hand.

Donna poured herself a glass of iced tea and sat down at the table with them. "What are you going to do?"

"Nothing," Roxanne replied.

"Don't you want to help them?" Donna asked.

"No."

Donna grinned and walked over to the table. Putting an arm around her granddaughter's neck, she said, "Just testing you."

Roxanne hugged her grandmother.

"Forget the wine, we need the hard stuff." Donna straightened, opened the liquor cabinet and pulled out a bottle of tequila.

Roxanne burst out laughing. "Is that your answer to everything?"

"It is. Especially since you girls are both over the age of twenty-one. Margaritas, anyone?" Donna then opened the refrigerator and brought out a bottle of margarita mix and limes. "I made myself a solemn promise. If I exercise every day, I can drink margaritas."

"Didn't you spend an hour at the gym this morning doing Pilates?"

"Just so I can have a cocktail," she said to Roxanne.

Portia shook her head. "Grandma, you're my hero."

Roxanne hugged her grandmother. "Mine, too."

"Then we're going to sit down, put our heads together and figure out what we can do to foil my DNA's contribution to the future." Donna pulled out the blender.

"Grams," Roxanne said, "At some point you have stop blaming yourself for Mom and Dad's decisions. Life is a crapshoot."

Portia jumped to her feet to retrieve ice from the freezer. She filled a bowl and handed it to Donna who dumped it into the blender, then added tequila and margarita mix. Roxanne stood and opened a cabinet and brought out the margarita glasses.

"What are our options?" Portia asked.

Donna thought hard for a moment. "Just ignore them. That irritates them the worst."

"Having my parents back in my life would bring up all the old anger, resentment and distrust. I don't need them."

"Then option two would be figuring out a way to get them to back off," Donna continued.

"Maybe if I accused them of stalking..." She doubted an accusation would stop them. They were too determined. "Is there an option three?"

"Pack up and move to Norway," Portia said.

"Paris," Donna said, "and you'd have a deal."

"London," Portia said. "I don't speak French."

"There's an island right in the middle of the Channel," Roxanne said with a laugh. "We could go there."

"What would you do?" Roxanne asked. She trusted her grandmother implicitly.

Donna pursed her lips. "Let your parents initiate all the drama. I think in the long run, it reflects badly on them and not you, no matter how hard they try to spin it otherwise."

Roxanne spun all the information through her mind. Maybe she needed to stop worrying that bad stuff was going to happen. After all, the endgame was building her business and making Nancy happy, not diving headfirst back into show business. Her bit parts were enough, and even those were becoming less and less appealing as they pulled her away from her true passion of genealogy.

Her grandmother took her hand. "What happens, happens. You have no control over your parents and what they think or do. All you have to do is act in the gracious manner you've cultivated all these years. Be classy. Be above the madness."

Roxanne closed her eyes. She would try, but with her parents on her back, it was hard to rise above it.

She just hoped her parents didn't interfere too much. She needed her head in the game so she didn't let everyone at *Celebrity Dance* down.

Chapter 3

Tristan Deveraux was tall and thin. He shared the same facial structure as Roxanne, but his mouth was tight and his eyes held an angry, challenging gleam as though daring the world to cross him. Though he wore a business suit and all his tattoos were covered except for the snake curling up the side of his neck, Nick knew he ordinarily dressed like a thug with gold chains around his neck, no shirt and lots of leather.

Nick had seen Tristan in his parents' restaurant in the past, but tonight Tristan had a look about him as he approached Nick, a small, pudgy man in tow.

"Nick Torres," Tristan said, keeping his voice low and pleasant. "Can I have a minute?"

"What can I help you with?" Nick said, annoyed at

being approached. Both of the men reeked of whiskey fumes.

Tristan said, “My sister is going to be working with you on *Celebrity Dance*. She’s a bit of a klutz, so I hope she doesn’t embarrass you too much.”

Nick was almost too surprised to answer. “I have no complaints.” He had no intention of telling this man, even though he acted as though he were still in high school, about anything that happened between him and Roxanne.

Tristan gave him a slight smile. “I hear you and your business partner are planning a revival of *Timbuktu*. I was hoping we could talk.”

“I make it a policy to not talk business in my parents’ restaurant. This is family time.” He considered calling security and having them eject Tristan, but the man was Roxanne’s brother. Her family was already a huge mess—he didn’t want to add more to the chaos. He said, “Make an appointment with my assistant.”

“I can do that.” Tristan touched an eyebrow in a mock salute. He turned and left, the pudgy man following close behind.

Nick took out his phone and called Mike. “Prepare yourself. Tristan Deveraux is planning to make an appointment to talk to us.”

Mike sighed. “What the hell did you agree to that for?”

“Roxanne. Not that she asked me to.”

The explanation seemed to appease Mike. “That doesn’t sound like fun. Any idea what the man wants?”

“He wants to talk about *Timbuktu*.”

“That’s still in the planning stages. If he wants a part, we’re a long way from casting.”

"I can't say. We'll just have to wait and find out."

"I've been doing some digging into the Deveraux family. They are a hot mess, especially with the IRS breathing down their backs."

And gossip like that got around. Image was everything in the industry. And his sister Nina was an expert at publicity and could certainly handle any bad press that came his way.

He didn't want to need her for that, though. Roxanne deserved to be in the spotlight for her own right—not because of her parents' bad business decisions.

"I'll let you know when Tristan calls," Mike said and then disconnected.

Manny Torres made his way through the restaurant toward Nick. He stopped at a few tables to chat briefly with the occupants. Luna el Sol had been a hangout for the Hollywood crowd for decades.

Manny finally reached his son and sat down. "Is that yahoo giving you trouble? He and his parents are loud, obnoxious and lousy tippers."

"How do you know they're lousy tippers?" Nick asked.

"I had two waitresses out sick with the flu. I pitched in and waited on his table. He stiffed me on a tip, and I'm a better waiter than a chef and I'm a great chef. And I own the restaurant. I found out from everybody, he and his parents tip lousy anyway, and complain about the service and the food." Manny pulled out a chair and sat down.

"You don't need tip money," Nick said.

"I don't keep my tips—I put them in the emergency slush fund for the staff. Terry Logan, one of the A-listers, was so happy with my service, he tipped me five large. Told me to buy your mother something pretty. I handed the money back to him and said, 'Sold.' Called your mother over and said, 'Hey, Grace, look what I bought for you.'"

Nick burst out laughing. "Was he amused?"

"Vastly," Manny said and slapped a hand on the table while he laughed loud enough that people at adjoining tables turned to look. Those who recognized him turned away smiling.

"Dad, when I grow up I want to be you."

"You already are." Manny rested his arms on the table. "So tell why you're here."

"Maybe I'm here for a good meal. I forgot my *Scooby-Doo* lunchbox at the house."

Manny glowered at Nick. "It's Tuesday night. You never come during the week while you're in rehearsal."

"Got me there," Nick said. "Roxanne Deveraux is a contestant on *Celebrity Dance*. And I think her brother wants a part in a play Mike and I are planning to revive. He has a reputation for being difficult to work with and I'm not sure I need the headache he'd generate."

"Maybe, but he's pretty talented. I've heard him sing and he has a great voice. What are you going to do?"

Nick didn't know. He didn't want to be a jerk about it, but he needed to protect his show and his reputation. "Roxanne doesn't want her family around. They ambushed her in the parking lot of the rehearsal studio and she was less than thrilled. They're pushing her to do a movie and she's not interested."

"I don't know about her siblings, but she seems to have a decent head on her shoulders. She could have gone off the deep end after she emancipated herself, but she went to school instead. She's a smart, talented, beautiful woman." Manny shook his head. "She appeals to everybody. She is going to be a great addition to *Celebrity Dance*."

Nick laughed. He couldn't argue with that assessment. "She's also funny and the biggest klutz in the world. My toes are never going to be the same." Roxanne had mangled a dance as simple as a waltz. He didn't think twenty hours a week of rehearsal was going to be enough for her.

"I'm sure you'll find a way to keep Roxanne's family drama out of the media and make this season work for all of the contestants," Manny said.

"I was sort of hoping you might have some ideas." Nick had always come to his father for advice.

"Not a one," Manny said. "You'll find a way." Manny clapped Nick on the shoulder. "You always do. You'll think of something."

"Keep your shoulders straight and your elbows up," Nick said. "Relax."

"I'm trying." Roxanne found it difficult to relax. She stumbled, but Nick caught her and eased her back into the flow of the dance. She tried hard not to step on his feet and at times she thought she was doing well, but then she'd lose her step.

"Step and glide," Nick said.

She did and managed a graceful turn. The eye of the camera followed her and she smiled for it. She'd grown up in front of thirty million viewers and seldom gave the camera a thought.

She managed to follow him for several more beats of the music.

"Keep your chin up," Nick said. "The waltz is considered the king of dances."

"Why not the queen of dances?" she stumbled but quickly righted herself.

"Because I didn't write the history of the waltz." He twirled her and smiled when she managed to avoid stepping on his foot.

She grinned at him, enjoying having this sexy, strong man's arms around her. "What else do you know about the waltz?"

"During the Regency period it was considered quite risqué."

"Wow. Who knew one dance could turn a whole period on its ear."

"Matrons from the period were known to swoon from the implied sexual innuendo of the waltz."

"Really?" she said. "There's a football field between us. I don't find anything sexy and risqué about the waltz."

"In Regency England, a man only danced a waltz with a woman he was serious about, sort of an announcement to society he was considering this woman for marriage."

"Are you considering me for marriage?"

"As a Regency gentleman looking at your prospects, you do have a healthy dowry. But for the most part, a Regency gentleman didn't consider a woman with brains a good catch."

She frowned. "Read a lot of Jane Austen?"

He laughed. "I didn't say Regency men were smart, but they were always looking to move up the ladder."

"Aren't we all."

"You knew what I was talking about all along, didn't you?" Nick grinned at her.

"Yes, but it was nice to know you paid attention in history class."

"The history of dance was a required class." Nick spun her and she followed his lead almost flawlessly.

She smiled happily. He spun her away and twirled her and she felt as though she were dancing on air.

Nick stepped back and clapped. "When you are focused on something other than your feet, you do great."

Heat flooded her cheeks. "Really."

"I would never lie to you about dancing."

Which made her wonder what he would lie about. "I appreciate that."

"We need to find a way to make you stop thinking about your feet."

When she'd been on *Family Time*, there would be moments when people would go off script and the whole routine would work brilliantly. Her costars had all been about fun and enjoying the moment. She needed to find a way to put herself in the moment so she stopped thinking about what her feet were supposed to do next.

"Let's do this again," Nick said, holding out his hand. "Trust me."

She took his hand and smiled at him. She almost felt graceful. The music restarted and she closed her eyes to avoid thinking about her feet. Don't think. Don't think.

Don't think. The mantra went round and round in her head. She took a step and landed wrong, sitting down hard on her butt. That hurt.

Nick grinned. "You fall very gracefully."

"I fall like a rock."

"A graceful rock." Nick held out his hand and helped her up.

Four hours later, she sat on a bench massaging her feet.

"You have an appointment with Wardrobe tomorrow at 2:00 p.m."

"I already put it in my phone. I didn't forget."

He grinned while he wiped his face with a towel. "Get a shower. I'm taking you to lunch."

"Someplace with pizza."

"Pizza sounds good."

She headed toward the locker room, relieved to be done with rehearsal for the day. Even though she was anxious to go home and get some work done for a client whose genealogy was already done. She just needed to put the finishing touches on the report and make it look pretty. She couldn't resist lunch with Nick.

Hollywood Boulevard was always busy. Nick parked in a lot behind the El Capitan Theater and he and Roxanne walked to the most famous street in Hollywood. Traffic on the street moved slowly while tourists snapped photos through the open windows of their cars. People on the sidewalks looked down at the row of stars beneath their feet, snapping photos and looking awed.

The day was pleasantly cool with a bright, sunny sky and no clouds overhead. Nick led her to the corner and they started walking down the Hollywood Walk of Fame. The bronze stars beneath her feet read like a who's who of old Hollywood.

"Look down," Nick ordered.

Roxanne did and found herself standing in front of Ginger Roger's star. She knelt down and rubbed Ginger's name. She was awed to find Ginger sharing space with Marilyn Monroe and Ozzy Osbourne with Judy Garland a few stars away in one direction and Bob Hope in the other.

"Where's Fred?" she asked.

"Down the block, a bit farther on." He pointed. "And later we can cross the street and visit Charlie Chaplin if you want."

He led her to Fred Astaire's star embedded in the sidewalk. She saw Ella Fitzgerald and Tim Conway's stars along with Gloria Swanson, Al Jolson and George M. Cohan—Hollywood royalty. Some of the names she didn't recognize, but they had small icons beneath their names letting her know they were involved in radio, movies, music or television.

"Did you bring me here deliberately?" Roxanne knelt down and patted Fred's star praying to the dance god that she would inherit his moves.

"I want you to get the dance vibe from the two greatest dancers in Hollywood history, as far as I'm concerned, and feed you pizza at the same time."

"Because I'm hungry?"

He pointed at the star. "Because you can dance. We're going to eat pizza at Combo's and stroll over Fred and Ginger's stars again and let you feel their moves." He swiveled his hips slightly and did a tiny jig. A passerby stopped to watch Nick, grinning. He snapped a quick photo and continued on.

Roxanne grabbed his hand. “Stop that. I’m hungry. We’ll dance later.”

Combo’s New York Pizzeria was flanked by the Guinness World Records Museum and a storefront selling tickets to tours of the superstars’ homes on one side and an empty retail place with a for-lease sign in the window on the other. At the end of the block, the Church of Scientology rose high into the sky.

They took their slices of pizza and sodas to a round sidewalk table with two aluminum chairs. Roxanne loved watching tourists. No one knew who she was, but a couple people seemed to recognize Nick.

“Your brother, Tristan, paid me a visit last night.” Nick took a bite of his pizza and watched her.

“I apologize,” she said, angry that Tristan had ambushed Nick. Tristan had been twelve when Roxanne made her break for freedom and sometimes she wondered if she should have found a way to save her siblings, too. Even though she’d only been sixteen at the time and could barely fend for herself, guilt still haunted her.

“What do you need to apologize for?” he asked.

She sighed. “The fact that he used our mutual DNA as an excuse to bother you.”

Nick shrugged. “No need. You had nothing to do with his actions.”

“How did he want to exploit you?”

“I didn’t give him a chance to try.”

No surprise, there. “What did you do?”

“I told him to make an appointment?” he asked, one

eyebrow rising. He paused for a long drink from his soda and studied her intently. "I know in one respect this is none of my business, but can you tell me what happened between you and your parents? Assuming you aren't violating any confidentiality agreements. I know it was in the industry publications, but not the real story about why you emancipated yourself."

Talking about her parents was painful. More than painful, excruciating. "You are my dance partner and I need to trust you." She paused, ordering her thoughts. "You can find out easily enough with a Google search. I started on *Family Time* when I was five. It ran for eleven years and the producers decided to end while still on top, especially with the children getting older and wanting their own space to grow."

Hollywood didn't have a good track record when it came to children in the business. Too many of them ended up dead because the industry put such a premium on things other than talent. "I made a good salary, especially as I got older. I wanted to get out of the business and go to college, but my parents had other plans for me." Plans that made her uncomfortable. Plans that made her worry their goals didn't coincide with hers. She wanted an education and they wanted their breadwinner back under their control.

"Parents are like that." Nick's tone was mild, nonconfrontational.

Roxanne sighed. She knew he meant well and she already knew that his experience with his parents was vastly different from hers. "My parents didn't want what was best for me, but what was best for them. The idea to emancipate myself was actually theirs. They wanted me to do this movie, but the studio was hesitating because I was still legally a child. To get around child labor laws, my parents talked to me about emancipation. The funny thing was, I was already thinking about it myself. I knew they wanted me to make this 'artistic' movie and thought they would still control me, but the movie had so many graphic sex scenes and nudity that I didn't want to be a part of it. Number one, just reading the screenplay made me uncomfortable. Number two, I enjoy making people laugh even though comedy is not my specialty. Unfortunately part of the emancipation also meant looking at my finances and my ability to support myself. My parents weren't expecting that."

"The government is like that," Nick said with a half smile as though he knew what was coming next.

Reliving a period that was one of the most painful times in her life, Roxanne took a deep breath, her pizza forgotten. "When I started on *Family Time*, I made $25,000 an episode over twenty-five episodes. A half million a year. By the time the show ended, I made $180,000 an episode and I was in every episode. Even with my parents acting as my agents and taking 15 percent, I should have had around $20 million in the bank. But when all the dust settled and the forensic accountants had a chance to look at my account, they found less than $2 million, and then the IRS got into the act, as well. And when the accountants really started looking at my money, they discovered a lot of irregularities."

"What kind of irregularities?" he asked, watching her intently as she spoke.

She drummed her fingers on the table. Talking about the situation made her nervous and vaguely disloyal to her family. "I understood I was the breadwinner for my family, but even when I was twelve I knew the gig would end." Few sitcoms lasted as long as hers did. "I planned for my education, but my parents squandered my money on questionable investments, bad business decisions and the high life. When the IRS got in the act, my parents tried to make it seem that I owed the back taxes. Fortunately for me, the government could see exactly what happened and went after my father." She remembered how her grandmother stepped in and told her she wasn't responsible for her parents' problems. They brought everything on themselves and she didn't have to bail them out.

"It must have been hard to see your parents in such a harsh light."

"What was harder was leaving Tristan and Portia behind. I still feel guilty I couldn't find a way to help them." Tristan was already in commercials and Portia was just starting out. Her parents would still have income. "I took what little money was left and ran. I had no intention of making that 'artistic' film no matter what they said trying to convince me. Their own greed gave me the way out. My grandmother…" Her grandmother was the best thing that ever happened to her. "…hired a financial advisor and he advised me on what to do. Grams and I moved to Berkeley and I went to school." That was the best decision she'd ever made.

Her parents had to know that her show could easily end and that getting more work for her would be harder because she wasn't a cute little apple-cheeked kid anymore. They should have saved their money. And Tristan was just like them, living in the moment.

"I read an article in *Variety* when they interviewed your parents," Nick said, "and they kept referring to you as that 'other daughter.'"

That hurt. She wanted to love her parents and wanted them to love her, but the veiled threats and insults had changed her.

"I couldn't be the daughter who would do anything for them, just so they keep up their lifestyle," she said.

Because there was so much scrutiny on them now from the government, her parents had been a lot more cautious with Portia's money. And Portia was careful herself. Unlike Tristan who couldn't seem to keep a penny in his pocket, Portia saved every cent she could with her eyes on UC Davis and veterinary school. And her parents still took their 15 percent of both without even trying to help Tristan be more responsible with his money.

"Thank you for trusting me with all that."

She leaned forward, wondering how to impress on him to stay away from her parents. "Your best bet is to stay away from them." She put every emphasis she could into her words.

He nodded. "I have every intention of doing so, but..."

She gave him a hard look. "But what?"

His fingers drummed a tattoo on the tabletop, his eyebrows scrunched up in thought.

Nick nodded. "Finish your pizza, I want to ask you something."

Her pizza was cold and she took a couple bites and set it aside. Her appetite was gone. "What do you want me to do?" she asked, half-fearful.

He smiled at her. "First off, how long does it take to do a genealogy?"

"There's no correct answer for that. The shortest time was a month and the longest was seven months. It all depends on how accessible the information is and how quickly I can find it. Why are you asking?"

"I've been thinking about doing a genealogy of my family for my siblings as a Christmas present. I know it's only May, but I like to plan ahead."

Relieved, she said, "I can do that."

"What do you charge?"

She thought quickly. She'd just finished a job for one client and only had one more. With the time frame he'd given her she could do this. "For you, no charge."

He held out his hand and shook hers. "That sounds reasonable. Done."

After lunch they strolled across the street for a quick visit to Charlie Chaplin and Walt Disney's stars. Roxanne had a fondness for Disney since the studio had produced her favorite animated film of all time, *Fantasia*.

"You know your way around," she said.

"When my sister Lola and I were kids, we used to pack up her keyboard and my tap shoes, and come down here to perform. She'd play music and I'd dance. And sometimes our brother Sebastian would come. He's a magician and can put on a show that totally enchants an audience. We made some pretty decent money. On a good day we'd take in a couple hundred dollars. By the time I was sixteen, I had enough money for my first car."

She liked that he knew the meaning of hard work. If she wasn't careful she would fall for this man. That would not be a good idea. His celebrity status would put her more into the spotlight and in her parents' sights.

"What was your first car?"

"I can see you're thinking it was some sort of exotic car like a foreign sports car."

"That did cross my mind." Her own first car had been a little Mercedes Roadster which she had adored. Not the most practical car, but she'd wanted it and she had the cash to get it after her finances recovered.

"I bought a Toyota Camry," he said.

She wanted to laugh, but good manners helped her hold it in. "You bought a mom car?" She tried to picture all six feet two inches of him crammed into a Camry.

"I needed something practical to drive around. I kept that car until I graduated from UCLA and moved to New York. Sold it then. Didn't need a car in the city."

She shivered. "I was in New York City a few times. It is one scary city." It had been loud and busy twenty-four hours a day.

He smiled. "I loved New York. I loved the energy, the brightness, the constant activity."

She could see he meant what he said. "I love Los Angeles," she said aware they'd arrived back at the parking lot. "At least you gave up being practical in your cars."

He grinned as he pointed the remote at his Range

Rover and unlocked it. "I can afford what I want now. Though you should see my twin brother's car collection. Daniel loves everything on four wheels. He has cars with names I can't even pronounce."

She'd met Daniel Torres briefly the morning the contestants for *Celebrity Dance* had been announced. He seemed like a nice man and she could see the brothers loved each other. That was nice. She wondered about the rest of his family. Were they as close as these two?

"I'm going to need some background info on your mother in order to research her genealogy chart," she said as he pulled into the parking lot where she'd left her Prius. "Why not come to my house tomorrow night? I'll make dinner and then we can get started on your genealogy research. I suggest we start with your mom. Finding out about your dad is going to take more work since he's from Brazil." She couldn't believe she had asked him to her house. She never invited anyone to her house. But it was too late to rescind the invitation.

Having someone at her house was intimate. Not like it was work. Nick was getting under her skin. She wasn't sure how to feel about it. As dance partners, they had to have a certain level of intimacy, but inviting him to her house was way over the line.

"That would be great."

"Yeah, about seven."

"I'm curious to see what you are like in your own territory."

How did she answer that? "I'll hide my panda slippers and Clippers sweatpants."

He laughed and took her hand. "This I have to see."

Chapter 4

Nick spent the morning at the gym with his brother Daniel. Because they were both on TV, they were deeply aware of their images.

Daniel ran on the treadmill while Nick worked his arms and shoulders on the free weights.

Afterward, they showered and went to their favorite corner café which offered the best enchiladas in Studio City.

"How are the wedding plans going?" Nick asked as he dug into the food.

"Do you know how crazy it is trying to plan a mobile wedding?"

"Not a clue," Nick said with a shake of his head.

"Getting married on a float on New Year's Day during the running of the Rose Parade has fun built into it, but I'd be just as happy eloping to Vegas." Daniel simply groaned. "Nina, Kenzie and Greer and her sisters are talking about a girls' weekend in New York for dress shopping. And florists all over the world are competing for the wedding bouquets and table arrangements at the reception. If we handle this right we don't have to pay for flowers. I saw the bill for the flowers for Nina's wedding so I'm cool with that."

Nick knew the wedding was going to be spectacular and flowers would play a prominent role—especially given Greer's profession.

Nick's phone rang. The display showed Levi Goldblum, top exec at the network. "I have to take this."

"Be in my office at two," Levi said and hung up.

"That was quick," Daniel said.

"Mr. Personality."

"Oh, Levi."

Nick pushed back from the table. "If I don't leave now, I'll be late." He reached into his pocket for his wallet.

Daniel held up a hand. "Don't worry about lunch, I'll get it."

Nick thanked his brother and headed for his car.

Levi Goldblum was a slim man, medium height, in his late twenties, dressed in an Italian suit that fit him like a glove. He sported a neatly trimmed beard, black-rimmed glasses, and reminded Nick of a well-dressed dork. Levi was hungry, ambitious and ruthless. Someday, he would be running the network from the penthouse office above him. Currently, he was senior vice-president of programming and he'd taken a chance on Nick's show on the strength of Nick's talent.

Levi's huge office was at the top of the network's thirty-story building and situated in a corner with wide views of Los Angeles. A huge desk dominated the room with a circular black leather sofa large enough to seat ten people in one corner, bookcases along one wall and a full bar and galley kitchen along the other wall.

"Sit," Levi ordered pointing at the sofa. "Coffee on the table."

Nick poured himself a cup of coffee and leaned back waiting while Levi paced back and forth with the suppressed energy of a hungry tiger.

"I don't like failures," Levi said.

Tell me a surprise. "Nobody does."

"Having Roxanne Deveraux on your show is a ratings coup. She hasn't really been in the public eye for over a decade and she's still in demand. She turns down more than she accepts and still everybody loves her even when she plays a corpse."

Nick felt confused. "What's the problem?"

"The bottom line is always money." Levi settled in the chair opposite Nick. "Her parents own the rights to a script for a TV movie which they sent to her. I had a chance to look it over and it's a good script. It's topical and sexy. It has a murder and the internet. All the things that make life worth living. No one hates to deal with crazy more than me. But I smell money and this—" Levi put a finger against his nose "—is never wrong."

Nick had to agree. Levi could smell money like a pig could smell truffles. When Nick and Mike had first shopped *Celebrity Dance* around the only person interested was Levi and Nick owed him for that chance at redemption. *Celebrity Dance* was a success and nothing said forgiveness like success.

"So what do you want from me?"

"The parents are playing hardball with the script and don't want to move forward with a development deal without Roxanne in the leading role. They aren't exactly wrong, she'd be great in it, even though we both know there are plenty of other actresses who'd jump at the part."

Nick raised his eyebrows. "Did you tell them that?"

Levi looked nonplussed. "What do you think? Nick, I don't like being backed in a corner—certainly by two wannabe hacks like Hannah and Eli Devereaux—but I want that script. Take Roxanne's pulse. See how she feels about doing the movie."

Nick already knew how she felt. "I'll talk to her, because I owe you, but I don't think she's really interested."

Levi was pragmatic. "Do your best. She's either going to say yes or say no. Just give it a try."

"And you'll accept her decision, whatever it is?"

Levi gave Nick a long look. "Number one, you won't owe me anymore. *Celebrity Dance* turned out a lot better than I expected. Trust me, your show will keep me on top for a couple more years."

Yeah. The life expectancy for someone in Levi's position was around ten years unless they had more gold mines in the wings. "I'll talk to her."

Roxanne would be hurt because she'd just started to trust him and he had the feeling she would see this as a betrayal, but he couldn't change what he couldn't change. Trust was a marketable commodity. It wasn't given easily or lightly.

He knew that compromise was the rule in this game. A lot of people had to be made happy. He only hoped she would be okay with him broaching the subject with her. He owed Levi for taking a chance on *Celebrity Dance*, so doing this favor for him was important.

"I know their history with their daughter and trust me, my sympathies are with Roxanne Deveraux, but..." Levi's voice trailed away as he frowned with whatever thought occurred to him.

Nick did understand. Show business was all about money, no matter how pretty it looked on the outside. God, he only hoped Roxanne remembered that and didn't blame him.

Levi sighed. "My hands are tied. And I'm not giving up on what I want without exhausting every option."

"I'm going to say this again, but I don't think she's ever going to agree to work with them." He knew she wouldn't quit *Celebrity Dance*. She'd probably find a way to break her ankle before she'd allow her parents to exploit her again.

"She signed a contract to help promote *Celebrity Dance*. She's a professional and will do what needs to be done."

"I can't do this to her," Nick said quietly. "Roxanne is a nice woman. It's not her fault her parents...are... difficult." *Difficult* was the only word he could say about them without sounding crude. Hell, he wanted to be her hero. He wanted to date her. Where the hell did that thought come from? Damn, he was in trouble. He couldn't get personal with her. That would break rules one through ten. Don't date a partner, ever.

"I know," Levi said. "I like Roxanne Deveraux, too. She's always been bankable. People look at her and remember her as that cute little girl with the smart lines on *Family Tree*. She can have any kind of future she wants in this business. Even I've thrown her a few roles throughout the years, but she always passed. Maybe her stint on *Celebrity Dance* means she's ready to step back into leading roles."

"I don't think so. Having to deal with Hannah and Eli isn't on her plate at the moment."

"Don't be so sure. Blood is thicker than water and I've seen some of the bitterest family breakups in this business healed with the right opportunity at the right time. I'm willing to throw her parents a lifeline in order to get her, but I'm not drowning so they can live."

"Maybe you better talk to Roxanne instead of me."

Levi smirked at Nick. "Not a chance."

"Chicken."

Levi laughed. "I'm vegan, that's why I like to save chickens. I'm sorry I have to put you in this position and I'm even sorrier Roxanne has barracuda for parents, but you can't tell anyone I said that. It will ruin my reputation."

Nick nodded. "My lips are zipped." Nick stood and they shook hands, his estimation of Levi's character went up a couple notches. "You like her, don't you?" Nick said as he walked to the door.

"One time," Levi said with a wistful expression on

his face, "she was the romantic fantasy of a pimply-faced boy."

"You just went to an uncomfortable place."

Levi laughed. "I realize I have the reputation of being a cold, heartless reptile, but once upon a time I had feelings."

"I think you still have a feeling or two."

"Don't tell anyone." Levi slapped Nick on the back, opened the door and grinned. "I'll be in touch." He closed the door.

Nick was surprised at Levi's honesty. Levi was a company man who made decisions based on company policy and kept his eye on the bottom line. With Roxanne, he thought Levi was still that pimply-faced boy in love with a beautiful, lovable TV star and Nick would work with that.

Nick nodded at Levi's assistant as he headed for the elevator. His dinner with Roxanne was going to be very uncomfortable.

Roxanne was almost in heaven over her dress for the first show. She stood in front of the mirror staring. The wardrobe mistress, Fay Benson, grinned at her. Fay was a tiny woman with impeccable taste. She'd studied fashion design in Paris, but brought her skills to Hollywood instead of working for one of the big fashion houses.

"The dress is beautiful and perfect on you." Fay stepped back to eye her critically.

Roxanne couldn't stop staring. *Ginger Rogers, eat your heart out.* Her gown wasn't an exact replica, but close. The strapless bodice hugged her tightly, showing off her toned shoulders and arms, but the full skirt of feathers danced around her legs like it had a life of its own. Instead of the original white, the gown was a deep scarlet.

"I love it." Nick had told her she would.

"Nick has terrific taste." Fay tweaked the dress around Roxanne's hips. "It's a little loose. You've lost weight."

"And here I thought little elves were holding it up."

"Some double-sided tape will take care of the girls." Fay winked at her. "Don't worry. I've never had an unplanned wardrobe malfunction."

"I've never had a wardrobe malfunction ever."

Fay laughed. "You've never needed one."

Roxanne trusted Fay and had worked with her before when she'd been nominated for an Emmy for costume design.

"Now that you're all grown up," Fay said walking around Roxanne, "I can really dress you. I've been dying to do so for years."

When Fay dressed her, she put Roxanne in elegant, age-appropriate clothes. In an industry where the right dress could make or break a woman's career, Roxanne was thankful to have Fay's vision.

She may not want to be a huge star anymore, but she didn't want to look ridiculous, either.

Hitting the right steps without falling on her face was worry enough.

"I thought what you did at sixteen took a lot of courage. Most sixteen-year-old kids don't know their butt from a hole in the ground, but you took control of your life and didn't go off the deep end, unlike some child stars I could name like Maddie, whose last name I can't remember, from *Maddie's Mad World*."

"Yeah, she was a hotbed of crazy."

"She still is," Fay said.

"I have *so* missed working with you."

"You need to stay on the show for the entire season. I want to see you win the grand prize."

Roxanne nodded hoping for the best.

The kitchen smelled wonderful. Roxanne peeked in the oven at the pot roast. Her grandmother chopped salad while Roxanne set the table.

She loved her huge country kitchen. Two sets of French doors opened to a brick patio, pool and spa. A fireplace dominated one wall with two chairs and a sofa flanking it. Over the fireplace hung a flat-screen TV which swung out to reveal the electronics set into the wall behind it. A snack bar separated the family room from the kitchen.

Her favorite colors were green and blue, and they were both reflected in the furnishings and kitchen where the walls were a peacock green contrasting with the stark white cabinets. A door next to the refrigerator led to a walk-through pantry and the formal dining area beyond.

"Do you want me to disappear for the evening?" Donna asked after she covered the salad bowl with plastic wrap and set it in the refrigerator.

Stunned for a moment, she had to think of her answer. Yes, she did, but knew it would be the wrong choice. "This is business, not romance," Roxanne said. "You don't have to leave."

"You like him."

Roxanne sighed. She was so busted. Impossible to keep much from her grandmother. Most of the time that was a good thing, but at the moment, not so much. "What's not to like. He's fun, personable, talented and..."

"Pretty to look at," her grandma half sang.

"...and nice. He likes to read."

"He's perfect. Start having babies with him today."

She felt herself flush. With embarrassment? The possibility? There was that. "We're not talking about this anymore," Roxanne said. "Did you get started researching his mother?"

Her grandmother liked to keep busy and had offered to help with Nick's project.

"I did," Donna said. "Grace was born in Philadelphia and grew up in Atlanta after her parents divorced. Her mother remarried, but not her father. Or at least not what I can find. He's quite interesting. Grace Torres's father was career air force. He served as a fighter pilot in Korea and Vietnam. He had quite a distinguished career. He retired after Vietnam and came out to California."

"That's great info, Grams, thanks." Roxanne could show Nick that she'd already found some terrific information on his mother.

"I think I'll call Portia and have dinner with her." Donna grinned.

"Really, you don't have to."

"If somebody doesn't do something about your love life, you'll never have one." She winked as she left, leaving Roxanne speechless.

Roxanne opened her front door to find Nick there. She caught her breath and couldn't help but smile at him. "I brought a red and a white," Nick said handing two bottles of wine to Roxanne.

"We're having pot roast and salad." She took the wine, touched by his gesture.

He looked very handsome in gray dress pants and dark blue shirt open at the throat. "How did you like your costume for the first show?"

"Oh, my God," Roxanne said. "The gown is so beautiful I didn't want take it off, but it still needed alterations. I had some containment issues."

He laughed as he followed her down the hall to the kitchen. "The nice thing about being the producer is I get to pick the stars' outfits, and the fact that Fay threatened me if I didn't assign you to her was a great incentive."

"Fay and I worked together on *Family Tree*." She put the white wine in the refrigerator to cool and searched for the cork puller in a drawer. She handed the bottle of red wine back to him.

"She told me. I tried to get her to tell me stories about you when you were on the show. She must like you. She didn't say a word." Nick uncorked the wine and she pulled out two wineglasses.

"I didn't behave badly in front of Fay. I'm not dumb."

Nick poured wine into her glass and then his. She led

him into the formal dining room where her charts and preliminary information were spread out over the table.

She forced herself to think about work and not him. He was distracting and captivating. "I have some information you will enjoy." Roxanne gestured at the dining table covered with charts, two open laptops and a dozen file folders. "My grandmother helps me and she started tracing your maternal grandfather. He was career air force."

"My grandfather was a car mechanic in Atlanta."

"No, your grandfather is Lionel Stanton. He served in Korea and the Vietnam war."

Nick stared at her as if she'd lost her mind.

Roxanne frowned. She glanced at the information spread out on the table. She found a marriage certificate for Leonore Burgess to Lionel Stanton and then the divorce papers dated four years later. She handed them to Nick.

He read through them quickly. "I didn't know. My mother never talked about this man. She only talks about Grandpa Al."

"Maybe she thought her father was dead." Roxanne rustled through a stack of certificates her grandmother had found and printed off one of the registries she used. "From what I see here, your grandmother—Leonore Burgess Stanton—divorced her husband after four years of marriage. Here is a second marriage certificate to Alfred Bridges. At that time your mother was three years old."

"She's never said a word," Nick said with a frown. "I wanted this to be a surprise." He gestured at the table.

"I think it's a bigger surprise than you thought," Roxanne said. "One thing about doing genealogy is all the secrets delving into the past uncovers."

"I wonder what other secrets my mother has."

She took a deep breath. She understood that this could be a painful process and sometimes people changed their mind. "Do you want to keep going or scrap the project?"

"I want to keep going."

"You'll need to be prepared. Let's eat dinner and we'll get back to this."

They sat at the kitchen table. Roxanne wasn't a great cook, but she did a few things really well and pot roast was one of her best dishes.

"I had a meeting with Levi Goldblum today." Nick helped himself to a generous helping of the food.

"I'm not going to like this, am I?" She took a deep breath, preparing herself. Bad news was going to happen. She could handle this. And from the glint in his beautiful eyes, she could tell he was upset. "Okay, right between the eyes."

"The situation isn't as bad as you think." He paused to think through what he was going to say. "Levi is interested in a television movie your parents want you to star in. He thinks the movie is the perfect vehicle for you."

"And of course, he smells the money." The situation could have been a lot worse. Levi could have insisted she reconcile with her parents.

Nick shrugged. "Show business."

Oh, she knew. "I always heard he was an…egotistic, narcissistic, money-grubbing pain in the butt. And I'm saying this as nicely as I can." She finished with what she hoped was a bedazzling smile. "Though he does have the 'nose.'"

Nick grinned at her. "He is all of those things, but he was a fan of *Family Tree*. He remembers you fondly."

"Really," she said. "I'm kind of surprised someone like him remembers me. He's inundated by people every day."

"He does remember you and can shoot your star into the stratosphere."

"They did send me the script and I glanced through it. Surprisingly enough it was good—lots of commercial appeal. But I don't want to work with them. I don't even want to be in the same building with them."

"From what I'm hearing, they want to move into producing and get away from agenting." Potentially there was more money in producing though it was a riskier investment.

"I have to think about this. I really like playing a corpse. The role is uncomplicated and all I really have to do is look dead and hold my breath."

"Don't you want to stretch yourself?"

"Holding your breath is hard and unnatural. Besides, I believe launching my own genealogy business is me stretching myself. Let's set this topic aside for the moment and eat."

"Everything smells delicious."

"I can't compete with your parents, but I do have a few dishes I can do well and pot roast is one of them." She spooned salad onto her plate and drizzled dressing across it. “So tell me, when did you know you wanted to dance?”

“From the first time I saw *Singin’ in the Rain* with Gene Kelly.”

“How old were you?”

“Six,” Nick replied. “My mom signed me up for dance lessons the very next day.”

“I can relate,” Roxanne offered. “I always wanted to be an actress. At least until it stopped being fun.” She’d been four when she told her parents she wanted to be on TV. She made her first commercial six months later. Six months after that she was cast for *Family Tree.*

“When did the change happen?”

“By the time I was eleven, I wanted to quit.”

“Why did your parents make you keep going?”

“Because they didn’t want to get real jobs. I was the moneymaker and they made sure I knew if I wasn’t working the family would starve.”

“What about their other clients?”

Roxanne shook her head sadly. “They only received a 15 percent management fee for their work, but as my parents they managed *all* of my money.”

“That’s a heavy burden for a kid.”

“A kid has no rights and guilt is a great control mechanism.” Even though she loved the people she worked with, she’d started to resent the hours she spent on the set. Even with the child labor limitations it was more than she wanted. “If not for my grandmother, I probably would have gone off the deep end. My grandmother sat me down and kept me busy with my studies so I didn’t have time to be depressed. My grandmother loves history and she made me love it, too." And that love had started her on her quest to find out more about her ancestors. "What a surprise when I found out I'm a direct descendant of Alexandre Dumas through one of his many mistresses." Nearly forty at last count.

"He was French. That's what they do."

Roxanne started laughing. Nick always seemed to know how to lighten a moment. She sobered a bit. "You seemed to just glaze over this thing with my parents."

"What can you do? Your parents are a fact of life."

"I don't want them back in my life." Roxanne felt guilty for not liking her parents. "They always make me feel like a commodity and not a daughter. And seeing what they've done to my brother and sister…"

"I think that's sad."

Roxanne just nodded. "I guess I should thank Levi for his enlightened self-interest."

"He's thinking about the bottom line."

Roxanne shrugged. "That's the Hollywood way."

They'd finished the rest of their meal with lighter small talk and Nick helped Roxanne clear the table. After setting the dishes in the sink, he rinsed and she placed them in the dishwasher.

"Show business can be so callous. There's a lot of ugliness in the background." Roxanne closed the dishwasher and stood with her hands on her hips. She studied Nick.

"I really like you and watching you have to rehash the past with your family is hard."

"Wow. Thank you." She felt oddly pleased. With

those words she was totally committed to *Celebrity Dance*. She wasn't going to let Nick down.

"Will you think about the movie?"

"How about if I think about thinking about it?"

Nick slid his hand on top of her hand. "Thank you."

Before she knew it she leaned in and didn't stop until she felt her lips meet his. His mouth was soft and yielding and his lips opened to her. His tongue slowly slid into her mouth and she felt his warmth and tasted his slightly minty breath. Her heart could have leapt from her chest. Their kiss was passionate yet soft. He moved his mouth over hers and she felt his hand move around her neck. She gave herself over and let him lead the way. For a few moments she thought their kiss would never end. She didn't want it to. Finally, he pulled back.

"Wow," he whispered.

Yeah, wow. She laughed. "I'm sorry about that."

"Don't be. I'm not."

"Well, thank you for being in my corner." God, she hoped she didn't sound as awkward as she felt.

No, that wasn't right. She wanted that kiss. She wanted him.

He leaned back and shrugged. "Not a hardship."

"I promise I'll think about it. I'll even read the script all the way through…" She let her words trail off.

He gave her a strange smile. "Thank you."

Roxanne stood. "Let's get back to work."

Chapter 5

The dress rehearsal was perfect. Roxanne didn't step on Nick's foot even once. She'd twirled and dipped with such perfection he could tell she was on a high. He watched the playback on the monitor. The dress moved beautifully. Nothing fell out that wasn't supposed to. Nick's tuxedo contrasted perfectly with her scarlet dress. She was going to be okay.

For the first time all the contestants were together. Nick and Roxanne had the number four slot out of ten.

Backstage, Roxanne sat watching a monitor as the audience streamed into the studio.

Nick sat next to her. "I don't want to bug you, but..."

She grinned at him. "I finished the script. And it's as good as I originally thought. But I don't know if it's good enough to tempt me. And making a decision is going to take longer."

"They've been calling Levi daily since I told him you'd read it. They're very brave to tackle Levi."

"They even leaked it to *Variety* that I'm planning my comeback project with this film."

"Ouch. Sorry about that."

She pointed at her brother as he walked into the studio. A woman reached for him and he stopped to autograph her shoulder, the point of the pen dipping down toward her breast. Nick frowned.

"Have you talked to my brother yet?"

"The appointment is next week, but I'm hoping something will come up between now and then so I'll be able to cancel."

Roxanne's parents entered and stopped to take selfies, as though they were royalty with various audience members. And from the tapping they did on their phone, Nick figured they were uploading the photos to Instagram. That annoyed him more than he thought it would.

Roxanne watched her parents, her lips tight with irritation.

The audience was finally seated. Cameras moved into position around the dance floor. The judges entered to the audience applause. Music was cued and the show started with Nancy, who acted as host, introducing the first set of contestants.

Roxanne had practiced her butt off and now that she was watching the first dancers, a sinking feeling settled in the pit of her stomach. No matter how much

Nick had rehearsed and praised her, she wasn't going to be able to top their performances, or even be in their neighborhood. And the fact that her parents were in the audience was also unsettling.

How had they even scored seats?

She watched the monitors. Each pair of dancers seemed flawless even though the judges pointed out the flaws in each performance. Panic rose in her. She glanced at Nick.

"You need to just take a moment and enjoy this," he said.

"Five gazillion people are watching this and my shoes are uncomfortable. I can't relax."

"Take deep breaths and clear your mind. Don't think about rabbits."

"What?" she asked.

"Don't think about rabbits."

"Why are we thinking about rabbits?" She didn't get it.

"It's a tactic to get you to stop thinking about dancing and divert your thoughts to rabbits."

"But you told me not to think about rabbits."

"What are you thinking about right now?" A smile spread across his face.

"Rabbits. I don't want to think about rabbits."

"Rabbits are cute, furry and loveable," Nick continued. "Don't think about them."

"Now that's all I can think of," Roxanne complained.

"I've done my job."

The third set of dancers completed their routine and faced the judges. Roxanne frowned. She couldn't get the thought of rabbits out of her head.

When their names were called Nick grabbed her hand. "Head up, shoulders straight. We're on. Smile."

The music started and he led her to the dance floor.

"I'm still thinking about rabbits when I..."

He grabbed her and pulled her into his arms. "Now, it's time to dance."

A smile spread across her face. She squared her shoulders and in the next moment she was whirled about.

One, two, three, step and slide. One, two, three, step and slide. Whirl. Whirl. She hadn't stepped on Nick's foot yet. Smile. Smile. Head up. Shoulders square. Step. Step. Step. Twirl. Smile.

Her dress swayed around her and she concentrated on Nick. He nodded at her. Okay, she was doing all right. Smile. Smile. Step. Step. Stay in step with the music.

And then the dance ended, the music trailing away. The audience clapped enthusiastically. She glanced at her parents and saw her mother frowning and shaking her head.

She was breathless. She hadn't stepped on Nick's foot once.

He turned her to face the three judges.

Emily Gray was a slim woman who had started her career with the San Francisco Ballet. William Eddings had been a dance instructor before heading to Broadway. According to Nick, William had taught him everything he needed to know about dance. Simon Pierce was a champion ballroom dancer.

"Well done," Emily said. "For a first dance it was passable." She nodded and smiled at Roxanne. "Your technique was good, but your moves lacked passion."

I didn't fall flat on my face, Roxanne thought.

"I agree," William Eddings said. "You were graceful..."

"I was?" Roxanne blurted out.

Nick hugged her. "You were."

William continued, "But like Emily said, you lacked passion. You acted distracted."

"I was thinking about rabbits," Roxanne said.

Simon Pierce looked confused. "Rabbits?"

Nick laughed. "I was trying to keep Roxanne from panicking. She has a tendency to overthink things."

The three judges laughed.

"Like another dancer I once worked with," William said with a pointed look at Nick.

"I love your dress," Emily said. "Very Ginger Rogers."

"I was trying to channel her, but I ended up channeling rabbits," Roxanne said with a glare at Nick.

Emily simply nodded.

Simon Pierce smiled at her. "You need to work on your movements. They need to be sharper and more crisp. You're this tall, beautiful woman and I know you can dance to match your body. You have a spark. You have presence."

Roxanne didn't know what to say. Nick took her hand and led her backstage to be confronted by Sophia Wills for the postdance interview.

"How do you feel?" Sophia asked.

"I got through the routine and I didn't fall on my face or grievously injure my partner."

Nick and Sophia laughed.

"Even though the judges felt you didn't convey the passion of the dance, you did look beautiful."

"I need to thank Fay Benson, who created this dress. She's an amazing designer."

Sophia looked surprised. "She did right by you. What do you have in store for next week?"

"My goals are not to fall, not to injure Nick and remember to smile and feel some passion."

Sophia touched her earbud. "The judges are ready with your score."

They turned to the monitor. Emily held up her scorecard—a five out of ten. William gave them a six. Simon held up a four.

"That's respectable," Nick said.

"I have a lot of improving to do."

Nick hugged her. She kissed his cheek, overwhelmed with the feelings inside her. She was happy she'd managed to not stumble, happy it was over. She had to do better next week. If she had to put in extra hours of rehearsal, she would. She wanted to please Nick, not embarrass him.

Nick guided her to the end of the room where the other dancers who'd already done their routines clustered in front of monitors to watch the remaining dancers.

Roxanne hated to take off the dress. She stood in front of the mirror in her dressing room for several minutes before removing it for jeans and a T-shirt.

Nick waited for her in the hallway. He leaned against the wall, arms crossed over his chest.

She was almost afraid to ask him, not sure she

wanted to know the answer. "You haven't told me yet your assessment of my dancing."

"You looked radiant in that dress. You kept in step with the music. You smiled. And the audience loved you."

"Really." Her mother hadn't loved her, Roxanne thought, remembering the frown.

"You could have been the crappiest dancer of the evening, but when you started talking about rabbits everyone in the audience laughed, including your parents. You were funny and you thanked Fay for designing your costume. Nobody does that."

"Fay did a wonderful job." Roxanne always gave people their due.

"You filled out the dress in all the right places and you believed in what you were doing."

Heat rushed to her cheeks at the compliment. "So what's next?"

"You missed last night's announcement of next week's theme. Iconic dances."

"I tried to pay attention," she admitted, "but I was so excited, my mind kept wandering."

"That's okay. I listened for you." He grinned and held out his hand.

"You already knew."

Nick laughed. "Guilty. I'll walk you to your car."

"What iconic dance are we doing?" she asked as he opened the door to the parking lot.

"I'll tell you tomorrow."

The parking lot was brightly lit. Other dancers lingered in the pools of light still elated by their performances. Their laughter floated across the lot.

Roxanne almost danced her way to her car, only to halt so suddenly, Nick bumped into her. Her mother and father leaned against her Prius, obviously waiting for her.

"That was a pretty dismal performance," Hannah Deveraux said caustically.

"For a first dance, she did just fine," Nick said in defense.

"Go away," Roxanne said. "I don't want to talk to you. Bye." She pointed the remote at her car to unlock the door.

"You're going to talk to us."

"No." Roxanne dug into her purse.

Her father stood up. Eli smiled at her. "I think this little feud has gone on long enough. We're here to ask for a truce."

"Really," Roxanne said, eyeing her father dubiously. "By telling me my dancing was dismal."

"Roxanne," her mother said impatiently.

"No." She found her phone.

"Mr. and Mrs. Deveraux," Nick said quietly, trying to be polite. It was well within his right to have them thrown off the lot, but he tried to be diplomatic for Roxanne's sake. "I don't think this is the time or the place for a scene."

Hannah's eyes narrowed. "This is between us and our daughter."

"You daughter doesn't want to talk to you."

"What they want," Roxanne said, "is for me to be back under their thumb, making them a lot of money and then all will be forgiven."

"Roxanne," Eli said, "you're always so dramatic."

"Doesn't mean I'm wrong."

Nick dug into his pocket for his phone. "If you don't get away from the car, I will call security."

Eli scoffed, "Is that all you're going to do?"

Nick shrugged. "I don't take out the trash."

Eli looked shocked, his overinflated ego clearly bruised. "This isn't over." He stepped away from the car and motioned to Hannah to do the same.

"I can make it over," Nick replied.

Eli grabbed Hannah's hand and they walked off.

"Are you okay?" Nick asked when her parents disappeared to the other side of the parking lot.

"I've been dealing with this for years. They're just more desperate than usual." She frowned.

"What are you going to do?"

"If I were really in danger, I'd hire security. But I don't think they have the guts to really push this." Roxanne watched from a distance as her parents backed their Escalade out of its parking spot and roared out of the lot.

Nick pulled her into his arms and kissed her gently. She smiled at him as she climbed into her car. "I'll see you tomorrow."

He grinned. "Bright and early."

She backed out of the parking spot and slowly drove away.

Portia waited for Roxanne. She puttered about the kitchen with their grandmother. Donna stood at the stove cooking bacon and Portia bent over the counter dipping two slices of bread stuffed with cream cheese into an egg mixture. From the scent, they were making stuffed French toast with bacon. Yum. Roxanne's favorite comfort food.

"We figured you'd be hungry when you got home," Donna Deveraux said after Roxanne dropped her purse on the sofa and found herself gliding into the kitchen.

"I wish you could have been there," Roxanne said to her sister.

"No, thank you. Then I would have had to sit by our parents. And the fact that I still live with them is enough for me," Portia said. "I watched the show with Grandma. You were gorgeous and not one wrong move. I don't care what the judges said, you were great."

Donna nodded in agreement as she set the bread lathered in egg mixture into the frying pan. The bread sizzled. "I was so proud of you."

"Mom told me I was dismal," Roxanne said.

"What does your mother know? She has the grace of a sloth," Donna said, flipping the bread and letting her bitterness at her daughter-in-law show. A bit of cream cheese dribbled out from between the layers.

Roxanne's mouth watered. She was ready to gobble up every heavenly morsel.

"When did Mom tell you this?" Portia asked.

"In the parking lot as I was trying to escape." Roxanne sat down at the kitchen table ready to pounce on the stuffed French toast the moment Donna set the first one down.

Portia pushed the plate of bacon toward Roxanne.

"They were waiting for you?" Portia asked, frowning.

"I hope skulking in parking lots doesn't become a habit with them." Roxanne grabbed two pieces of bacon and munched on them while waiting for her grandmother to finish cooking. "I'm trying to keep my Daddy and Mama drama away from *Celebrity Dance*. I don't want to draw attention to it by asking that they be banned from the studio lot."

"How do you feel?" Donna asked, tactfully changing the subject. "Notwithstanding Hannah's comment. How do you feel about your performance?" She placed a plate of French toast on the table.

Roxanne tried to resist spearing it, but Portia slid the plate toward her. Roxanne pushed the bread onto her plate and reached for the maple syrup. "I felt alive." She cut into the toast and cream cheese oozed out, mixing with the syrup. The food was heaven in her mouth. She closed her eyes and let the smooth flavors romance her tongue. The same tongue she'd shared with Nick less than an hour ago. A thrill of desire radiated through her. She almost wished she'd brought him home with her, but she'd needed down time more.

"The camera has always been your friend even when you're pretending to be dead," Portia said.

Donna set more French toast on the table. Portia sat and grabbed her own, liberally buttering it and pouring syrup over the crusty brown slices. She looked up and saw Roxanne staring at her with raised eyebrows.

"What?" Porta said crisply. "I worked out for three hours today. I've earned the carbs."

Roxanne hid her smile. "When I walked away from the business, I didn't think I'd miss it," she admitted. "I still had my bit parts to fulfill the occasional acting itch, but being in the spotlight…"

She hadn't walked away from a career as much as she'd walked away from her future. She'd realized she'd never have a future while her parents controlled it. And now she was back in control and looking forward to a future again, a future of her own making.

"You were able to walk away because you had balance in your life," Donna said.

"I had balance in my life because of you," Roxanne said.

Donna simply smiled.

"How did Dad end up being so different from you?" Roxanne asked, unable to believe this woman was her father's mother. She was so different, so down to earth.

Donna paused with her fork halfway to her mouth while she gave Roxanne a long look. "The biggest mistake I ever made was letting my ex-husband take your father away from me. I thought Eli would be better off with his father. He always had money. I thought he'd be a better parent. Besides, I had no skills and no job prospects. And his lawyer was sleazier than mine. Little did I know my ex was a con artist when I thought he was a respectable businessman—a financial advisor who helped widows plan for their future. Instead he was stealing their money."

Roxanne only nodded. Her father had learned his own father's lessons well. He'd stolen from her and she would never forgive him. And her mother had made no objection, made no effort to protect Roxanne.

They finished eating. Roxanne cleared the table, putting the dishes in the dishwasher while Portia cleaned the stove. Their grandmother wiped down the sticky table.

Portia opened a bottle of wine and sat next to Roxanne in front of the fire, glasses in their hands. Donna had gone to bed citing that it was way past her bedtime, though Roxanne knew her grandmother could outlast them anytime she wanted.

"You looked pretty cozy with Nick." Portia adjusted the gas fire until it was just embers.

"We're supposed to look cozy. That's the whole point of the waltz." Heat flamed across Roxanne's cheeks as she remembered the kiss in the parking lot after her parents' departure.

"Something happened, didn't it?" Portia studied her sister, eyes narrowed with suspicion.

She should have known she couldn't keep a secret from her sister. She was Donna Junior and could almost smell intrigue. But was Roxanne comfortable talking about Nick? Even to Portia? She liked him a lot and he made her feel safe. She never really trusted herself to have more than a surface relationship with a man. Most of the time, they liked her for what she was, not who she was. Nick seemed to be just the opposite—and he certainly didn't need her for her fame—but still that trust was hard to come by. Yet she seemed unable to stop herself from liking him. Maybe because they were partners. Partners who had to touch each other a lot. "You always did have an eagle eye."

"So give it up," Portia pressed.

"He kissed me." Roxanne half closed her eyes. The feel of his lips on hers had sent feelings through her she wasn't certain she wanted to examine. Her heart started to race and even her palms got sweaty. She was like a teenaged girl in the throes of her first crush. She felt stupid as well as giddy. Not a good combination as far as she was concerned.

"Your first kiss with Nick," Portia said, her tone awed.

"Actually, it's the second kiss."

Portia smacked her on the arm. "And you didn't tell me! Shame on you. You broke the sister code."

Roxanne laughed. "Only because I knew you'd hit me."

"Do you think getting involved with your partner is a good thing?"

"I'm not involved with Nick. We shared two kisses. Sometimes a kiss is just a kiss. No strings attached. And that's just how I'm thinking about it. Don't want to talk about it anymore."

Portia eyed her sister, a dubious expression on her face. "I want to talk about this kiss."

Roxanne waved her hands in front of her. "I don't have the words."

"How can you not have the words when a man who looks that fine kisses you?"

"Because he is that fine." Roxanne's words ended on a sigh.

"You sound like you don't think an attractive man would find you appealing."

Roxanne shook her head. "It's not that. It's..." Her voice trailed away while she searched for the words. "I'm juggling a lot of things. I don't think I can handle the romance ball. Between the two of us, we've dated our share of people in the business. Being involved with him is not a good bet."

"Are you already planning *the* great love affair?"

"No, I'm planning my next dance." Roxanne finished her wine. "I'm going to bed." In the face of Portia's onslaught her best tactic was to retreat. There was a lock on her bedroom door and she wasn't afraid to use it.

"Yeah, I guess it's time for me to head home." Portia pushed herself to her feet.

"No. It's nearly midnight. You've already had two glasses of wine, you're staying here. I'll hide your keys if I have to."

Portia grinned. "You don't have to talk me into staying. Just make sure I'm up at six. I have a photo shoot in the Valley."

"For who?"

"Him Magazine."

"Does that mean you're going to be doing stupid poses in revealing lingerie?"

"Yeah, but they're paying me a lot of money to do it."

"How much?" Roxanne asked curiously. No one had ever asked her to pose for lingerie. Not that she would, but, hey, it would be nice to be asked.

Portia held up three fingers. "Enough for three semesters of vet school."

"I told you I'd pay for your schooling."

Portia kissed Roxanne on the cheek. "If I take money from you, I'll just be like our parents. As much as I appreciate the offer, the answer is still no." Portia yawned. "Besides you're my role model. You've paid for everything you have. I intend to do the same." She stood and stretched, yawning again.

"It's not like I'm investing in yak farming. This is an investment in you. In your future."

"You know I love animals. I might want to buy a yak farm."

Roxanne laughed. "Now you want to save yaks!"

"Good night, sister dear." She headed for the guest room. "The yak savior is taking her dreams of salvation to bed."

Roxanne turned off the gas fire, collected the two wineglasses and put the half-empty bottle of wine back in the wine cooler. As she turned off the lights, she thought about Nick's kiss and the way he made her feel. She couldn't tell Portia about the way his arms around her left her feeling.

She just needed to get through this season of *Celebrity Dance* and then she could go back to her relatively peaceful life.

Chapter 6

Nick stood in front of the flat-screen TV hanging on the kitchen wall reviewing Roxanne's dance routine. His brother Sebastian sat at the kitchen able, decks of cards spread out in front of him.

"What do you think of my new card trick?" Sebastian asked.

Nick hadn't been paying attention, but didn't want to let his older brother know that. "It's great."

"You aren't watching. It's so great, you didn't even notice. I've been sitting here for fifteen minutes pretty much having a conversation with myself."

Nick glanced at his brother. Sebastian was a slim, elegant man with close-cropped hair and a nicely trimmed beard. He fanned a deck of cards for Nick to look at and then he fanned the deck the other way and all the cards changed to aces, black aces interspersed with red aces in all four suits.

Sebastian was a sleight-of-hand card magician who plied his tricks at the Magic Castle on weekends when he tended bar there. Sebastian had always been interested in card tricks starting with a Christmas gift when he'd been four years old. Since then, his focus had been on what he could do to dazzle an audience with cards. He had some pretty interesting sleight of hand tricks.

"That bad, huh," Sebastian continued, his tone casual.

"No. No. I'm just…thinking." Thinking about Roxanne Deveraux and trying not to think about their second kiss. The first kiss between them had rocked his world. The second was a tsunami of emotions.

"What are you thinking about?" Sebastian had never been one to sneak up on a subject. He was always direct and to the point. "What's going on, Nick? I've never known you to be so distracted. Is that gorgeous-as-sin Roxanne Deveraux the reason for your distraction?"

Nick turned back toward the TV, refusing to answer his brother, his gaze glued to Roxanne in her red dress and the look of total delight on her face as she moved through the routine. She had been graceful. Never once stumbled or stepped on his feet. She'd kept her head up, shoulders and back straight and remembered to smile. He could see why the judges thought she lacked passion. He knew she'd been so nervous that her only thought had been getting through the routine without falling and making a fool of herself.

"Having girl troubles?" Sebastian asked curiously.

"Though I've never known you to have those unless you consider fighting them off a problem. Unless you count Margo Kirby. She was a problem waiting to happen."

"And because of her, I'm in Los Angeles instead of New York." Nick had been bitter at first. Margo had done her best to blacken his reputation. Los Angeles represented a new beginning for him.

"If you hadn't been here, you would never have met Roxanne."

Leave it to Sebastian to figure things out. He liked her.

"You've watched that dance sequence about twenty times so far."

Nick glanced at his brother. "I suppose I am having woman trouble, but not the way you think."

"I can think up some pretty interesting scenarios, but this is sounding intriguing." Sebastian spread the cards across the tabletop. The card faces had returned to their normal appearances of four suits and thirteen cards each. "Do tell your big brother about your problems."

"Roxanne isn't the problem so much as her parents are."

"Ah, the famous or infamous, depending on your point of view, Eli and Hannah Deveraux." Sebastian started putting all the decks back in the boxes.

"Sounds like you've had a run-in with them before, too."

"Not them. Their son." Distaste showed on Sebastian's face. "Baby-man."

"What did baby-man do?"

"He came to the Magic Castle with a woman he wanted to impress."

"You didn't have to show him you are a Golden Gloves winner."

"No," Sebastian said with a laugh. "That would have been too much fun. This woman obviously wasn't interested in him, and that put him in a snit. He got loud and obnoxious and we had the distinct pleasure of kicking him out, and he did not go gently into the night."

"Sounds like he got what he needed."

"I've met both Portia and Roxanne. They are always polite and gracious. What happened to Tristan?"

Nick shrugged. Like he would know? His parents would never put up with bad behavior from any of his siblings. There were seven of them. No one challenged Grace and Manny's rule with their iron hands encased in velvet gloves.

"He's persona non grata at the Castle." Sebastian laughed. "Did you know there's a website dedicated to keeping tabs on him and a list of all the places Tristan is no longer welcome?"

Nick stared at his brother. "You're kidding, right?" He'd lived in New York way too long.

"I know two women who check the list regularly to make sure they don't run into him."

"It sounds like the type of publicity ploy Nina would scheme up."

"Don't let our sister hear you say that. Hannah and Eli offered her a job helping one of their problem clients, but Nina didn't like them or their client and turned them down flat."

Nick knew Nina was the best at publicity but didn't know that she'd turned down the Deveraux family as clients. But she was a smart cookie and she would never compromise her own ethics to work for people she didn't like.

"They're such attention whores. If you really want to annoy them, ignore them," Sebastian offered. "It's so much more fun."

His brow quirked at Sebastian's snark. "Temper, temper, brother. Who do you think has the mean streak? Grace or Manny?"

Sebastian thought for a moment. "Pops has the mean streak and Nina inherited it from him."

"And you, too," Nick said.

"But I'm never cruel. And I'm only mean to people who deserve it."

"That's what you call it." Nick was seldom mean. He had to deal with divas of both genders all the time and diplomacy was second nature to him. He'd developed those skills mediating all the quarrels between his siblings when they'd been kids.

Sebastian's eyebrows rose. "You act like I should be ashamed."

"Oh, no," Nick said. "Shame is not an inherited family trait." There had been times during their childhood when a couple of his siblings should have been ashamed. "We are Torreses and shame is not done."

Sebastian didn't answer. He stacked his boxes of cards.

"So what you're telling me," Nick continued, "is to ignore Hannah and Eli because it irritates them."

"And keep grooming Roxanne," Sebastian said. "She has star quality. She had star quality as a kid and she has it now, because I've seen you with better dancers. If last night had been an elimination show, she would have been gone, but the audience loved her and gave her a pass. Keep the audience loving her so much she could fall down and break an ankle and still not get voted off."

Nick could do that. Besides, he liked the feel of her in his arms. "I like dancing with her."

"Then just fall in love with her and be done with it," Sebastian said with a low chuckle.

Nick didn't think he was too far from falling in love with her already.

Roxanne woke with a start.

Portia shook her again. "Wake up. Wake up."

"What?" She threw her pillow at her sister, who ducked.

"Wake up." She thrust her Mac laptop at Roxanne. "You have to see this."

Roxanne rubbed her eyes and glanced at the clock. "It's six o'clock in the morning. I don't have to be at the studio until nine."

"You have to be awake now." Portia gestured at the laptop.

Roxanne settled the Mac across her lap. "What am I looking at?"

"Read the headline." Portia shoved Roxanne over and sat down next to her. She pointed at the headline. Nicholas Torres Caught Canoodling With Dance Partner.

"What?" Roxanne said as she scrolled down to read the article.

A video popped up showing her arguing with her

parents. She watched the whole scene and then as her parents walked off, she turned to Nick. They talked for a few moments and as her parents' SUV squealed out of the lot, he kissed her.

The kiss lasted long enough not to be a friend-to-friend type. As she watched herself, her arms slid around his neck and pulled him tight against her. The naked desire on both their faces startled her as the unknown cameraperson zoomed in tight on their lips and the way his one hand gently ran down the side of her breast.

"Oh, no." The video ended and she started it again. "Who did this?"

"I wouldn't be surprised if we dug a little deeper, Mom and Dad set you up. They probably made a boat load of cash selling this to TMZ."

"I doubt that. TMZ doesn't pay much." Roxanne played the video again. The betrayal hurt. They'd plastered the feud with her on the internet and now they were hurting Nick.

"They don't care," Portia said, disgust in her voice. "And I don't care. I'm done with them. Once my contract with them is over, I'm gone. I've decided it's time for me to get an education."

"They'll make life as difficult for you as they have for me."

Portia shook her head. "You survived and I will, too."

"I was sixteen years old and looked like the victim because I'm way better at playing the victim than you ever will be." Roxanne didn't mean to sound smug, but the truth was the truth. When Portia was in front of the camera, she was always Portia. Roxanne could be whoever she needed to be on camera.

"I can play the victim. We had the same acting coach." In a burst of restless energy, Portia jumped up and started pacing back and forth. "This is not good. Not good at all. Now is the time, we need to get you a publicist."

"Yeah," Roxanne said pushing the blankets aside. "I need to call Nick." What was her parents' endgame?

She reached for her phone. At the same time, it rang.

"Nick," she said.

"Did you see the video of our kiss?"

"Oh, yes," she said glancing at the computer.

"Do you think this is war?" She didn't add the kind of war that made a show or sank it. People tuned in to watch shows for the hookups and *Celebrity Dance* was no different.

"I think it's a skirmish."

"I'll be there."

He disconnected.

Roxanne sighed and pulled herself out of bed. While Portia glowered at the computer, Roxanne took a shower and dressed for rehearsal.

Nick paced back and forth across the dance floor. He was annoyed, but not surprised.

"I don't want my romance plastered across the media like my brother's romance with Greer." Greer and Daniel had been tabloid fodder for months.

"Is this a romance?" Nancy, who sat on a stool with her laptop on her lap, asked with a gesture at the screen.

"If it is a romance, I still don't want anybody in my business."

Nancy laughed. "Honey, you're a celebrity. Everyone's in your business. You know that. We need to figure out a way to use it."

Nick frowned. Mike opened the door and stepped into the dance studio, his phone to his ear. He disconnected and put his phone in his jacket pocket.

"Can we do anything about the video?" Nick asked.

"You know we can't, Nick. You know the breaks. Since the video was taken in a public place, whoever took it didn't need your permission."

"Do we even know who took the video?" Nancy closed her laptop with a snap, a frown on her face.

"Not a clue, but I think we can all guess who might be behind it." Nick said. "I don't understand why they would post the video of them arguing since it doesn't show them in a positive light and I think our kiss is the most interesting part of it."

"Because," Nancy said with a shrug, "publicity is publicity, good or bad. They left the argument in because it shows the context of the kiss. Mom and Dad are victims and Nicky is the bad boy who's corrupting their little girl. Never mind that their little girl can't stand them."

The door to the studio opened and Roxanne walked in. She looked a little disheveled, but still beautiful and Nick felt his blood begin to race.

"Good morning," Roxanne said.

"You doing okay since the video broke?" Nancy put her laptop into a briefcase and pulled out her iPad.

"We'll ignore the video," Roxanne said. She sat down on a chair.

Nancy said, "You're going to need to do an interview with why you broke off from your parents."

"I'll think about it. But if we ignore the video, that would anger my parents and I always go for what angers them most."

"Your parents are looking for a life raft," Nick said, "and it's got your name all over it. They are desperate people who might start manufacturing things about you."

"They've been doing that for years," Roxanne said. "I've heard the gossip about what they think could be wrong with me. *Why don't we get her a psychiatrist? Why don't we get her a witch doctor? Or get her on Dr. Phil?*"

"What?" Nick asked. "Are you serious?"

"Not about the witch doctor, though sometimes Portia exaggerates," Roxanne said with a nervous laugh. "I just can't see my parents wading through the jungles in Guatemala looking for one. They say these things in front of Portia knowing she'll tell me. It's very passive-aggressive."

"Aren't you afraid the public is going to think you're callous?" Nancy asked.

Roxanne shrugged. "You know the public is going to think what the public is going to think. All I know to do is protect myself. The funny thing, I love my parents. But they don't love me except for what I can do for them and that hurts. I spent a lot of time in therapy figuring out my relationship with them. I've dealt with the issue and I've moved on. They're stuck in some sort of repeat pattern that makes no sense to me."

"Can we announce you've been in therapy and have been for a number of years due to their mistreatment?"

Roxanne paused to think. "No. I think if I make some sort of official announcement about being in therapy, that will add more fuel. They can build on that and say look at this epic fail on my part and now I play corpses."

Nick held up a hand. "Executive decision. No announcement about her therapy. No comment on the kiss. Sometimes a kiss is just a kiss..."

"If you say so," Nancy muttered though she didn't look convinced.

Nick shot her an amused look and repeated, "Sometimes a kiss is just a kiss." Even when it wasn't.

He glanced at Roxanne and saw a blush grow over her cheeks. The kiss had been something more, but he wasn't going to admit that to Nancy. "Now, we need to start our rehearsal. The preshow interview is at ten and Roxanne has a wardrobe appointment with Fay right after lunch."

Roxanne took her sandals off and put on her dance shoes. "I'm ready," she announced. She stood, twirled and suddenly looked radiant.

Nancy kissed Roxanne on the cheek and left with her husband. Mike gave Nick a long, thoughtful look before opening the door for his wife and waving her through.

"I owe you an apology," Roxanne said.

"What for?"

"For casting you as the lead in my family's psychodrama."

He burst out laughing. “That’s kind of funny.” He held out a hand. He’d tried to minimize the stress on Roxanne.

“Thanks for being a good sport,” she said earnestly. “But are you really okay? My parents are difficult to deal with on a good day. And you’re in their line of sight now.”

“If push comes to shove, I can sic the family Torres on them.” Thinking about his mother in combat with her mother made him smile. Grace Torres was a lion and Hannah was the baby gazelle. There would be no contest. “I just picture my mother taking on your mother and we’re going to need the SWAT team.”

“I have them on speed dial.”

He kissed her on the cheek. Her skin was still as soft as it had been the night before and the scent of her perfume was a subtle citrus. “Me, too.”

Chapter 7

Roxanne pulled into her driveway to find her brother's silver Porsche already parked in it. She parked to one side, annoyed at him for hogging her driveway.

"What are you doing here?" she asked her brother, wondering how he got past the guard at the gate who was supposed to call her for visitors not on her allowed list.

Tristan Deveraux was a handsome man, tall and lean with muscles that bulged beneath the sleeves of his white T-shirt. He lounged on the porch swing dressed in jeans and a T-shirt. He held a can of beer in hand. A six-pack minus two cans sat on the porch next to him. "Can't I visit my sister?"

She glared at him. "Normally you come with motive and criticism in hand."

"Why can't you just cooperate?"

She stood at the door with no intention of opening it and letting him in. "Because I did my time. I just want to live my own life."

"We're your family and you're obligated to help us."

"No, I'm not. You're a grown man. It's time you made your own way in the world and they made their own way in the world. I refused to be tethered to them for the rest of my life."

"Ooh. Tough love, sis." He crumpled the empty beer can and grabbed another, jerking it loose from its companions.

"Like I said, I'm done." If they had understood how uncomfortable she'd been with the movie they wanted her to do back when she was sixteen, they might not be at this impasse. She loved her parents because they were her parents, but she didn't like them.

She waited with one hand resting on her hip.

"Mom and Dad are in really deep trouble. They need us. They need you."

"Other than the IRS, what other trouble could they be in?"

"They're bleeding clients. The word has gotten out about their IRS problems. If they can't handle their money properly, clients won't trust them to handle their careers. You know as well as anyone that image and reputation are sacred in Hollywood."

Roxanne shook her head emphatically. "I was perfectly fine with you bad-mouthing me and making me the villain. I never said anything and went on with my life. And now that I'm stepping back into the public eye you want me to be part of your little gang again. No."

Tristan frowned. "You played a corpse on your last TV appearance."

"So what? I was paid. I'm a working actor." She could offer her brother money, but what he really liked was the fame. In a weird way, the money was almost irrelevant except for the fact the IRS wanted their share and her father seemed to think he didn't have to pay taxes.

Tristan liked the money because of what it bought for him. He liked the women who chased after him. He enjoyed the preferential treatment. He would love it if he didn't have to work so hard. He thought he was entitled. His fame meant he mattered, that he was important.

"I'm being written out of my show," Tristan went on. "This coming season is my last and my contract isn't going to be renewed. In fact, I doubt I'll last beyond Christmas." He sounded almost sad despite the fact he truly hated the medical drama where he played a doctor, and had said so all too often in too many words.

"Maybe you shouldn't have bad-mouthed your show, your director, your producer, the network and your costars. Just saying."

He shrugged.

In the beginning, she missed being fawned over, treated as being special, but she found out later that walking into the grocery store anonymously was a bit of heaven. She didn't have to worry about being criticized for not wearing makeup. No one would question her purchase of a box of Twinkies and wonder if she would fit into her evening dress for whatever awards show or premier she would be attending. She didn't miss people picking through her trash. Though being anonymous was enjoyable, she still missed the limelight on occasion.

Of course that was going to change now that she was on *Celebrity Dance*, but some things couldn't be helped.

"Go home, Tristan."

"You help Portia. Why not help me?"

"Portia knows what she wants. She's willing to put up with all of you in order to attain her goal."

Tristan's eyes took on a nasty gleam. "How do you know she's not conning you?"

"For the simple reason that when I asked her if she would allow me to pay for vet school outright, she said no." And Portia stuck to her refusal. No argument Roxanne used changed her mind. "You put your argument out there," Roxanne said, "and I gave you my answer."

Tristan sighed. "This isn't over, Roxanne."

"I know. Tell me something. What do you want out of all of this? You're not a happy man." She knew what Portia wanted and what her parents wanted, but she had no idea what her brother wanted. "The money, the fame, the whatever, isn't enough. I can see you're not satisfied. What do you want? You're not a bad actor when you focus more on your craft than your fame."

He didn't answer. Instead he trotted down the porch steps and headed toward his car. He paused with one hand on the door. He glanced back at her and repeated. "This isn't over, sis."

"Of course it isn't," Roxanne muttered as she inserted her key into the lock.

The door swung open and Portia peered out. "Is he gone yet?"

Tristan backed his Porsche out of the driveway. "Almost."

Roxanne entered, closed the door and locked it. Portia kept herself out of view. She held her phone in one hand.

"Has he been here long?" Roxanne asked.

"Over an hour." Portia led the way back into the kitchen. "I was prepared to call security if he made himself too obnoxious."

"I'm not worried about Tristan." Portia set her purse on the counter and opened the refrigerator. Her stomach growled, "Deep down inside, he thinks he can change my mind about reconciling with Mom and Dad."

"Not happening."

"He doesn't know you very well, does he?" Portia laughed.

"He knows me," Roxanne said, pulling out sandwich meat, mayo, lettuce and a tomato. "He's just not willing to acknowledge that I have good reasons for my actions."

"I'm part of this little game, too," Portia said, handing her the loaf of bread from the bread box.

"No, you work because it's a means to an end. Sort of like waiting tables. You have your eye on the golden ring and nothing is going to deter you."

Portia shrugged. She sat on a bar stool. Her laptop was open and a genealogy chart lay to one side. She'd obviously been working on Nick's mother.

"Tristan just wants to be famous," Roxanne said as

she built her sandwich. She grabbed an ice-cold soda from the fridge and sat down next to Portia.

"He doesn't even want to work hard to be famous. He wants fame to pick him up at the house and deliver him to where he needs to be." Portia pushed her laptop and the chart away and leaned against the snack counter with her arms folded across her chest, elbows on the counter.

"No, I don't think that's really what he wants. There's more somewhere inside of him. He's not happy, Portia. He's a man who seems determined to self-destruct." His bad-boy behavior was a shout out for something.

How had her family turned out to be so dysfunctional? When had this all started? Had it been when she'd been cast in *Family Tree*, or earlier and she just hadn't seen it.

She could see on Portia's face that she knew something. "What?"

Portia looked away.

"You have to tell me," Roxanne pushed.

"About a year ago when he moved into his new man cave, I helped pack and I found some books hidden under his bed. They were on environmental engineering."

"Really?" Roxanne was almost too astonished to think up something else.

Portia nodded. "Yes."

"Color me surprised. Did you ask him about it?"

"He blew me off saying it was a gag gift and to let it go."

Roxanne pondered Portia's revelation. "Interesting."

"That's your I'm-up-to-something face," Portia said.

"Maybe I'll make him an offer he can't refuse."

"Entailing what?" Portia frowned.

Roxanne thought for a second. "California has a university for everything. I should be able to find out something about environmental engineering."

"University of California Riverside has an environmental engineering program."

Roxanne's eyebrows rose. "You've been busy."

"He's our brother and I love him even though he's a jerk most of the time."

"He's a jerk because he's miserable. And he's too immature to give up the trappings of fame yet."

"How are we going to help him?"

Thoughts tumbled over and around in Roxanne's mind. "He needs to hit rock bottom and not have something to cushion him."

"He's getting kicked off his show, isn't that enough?"

Roxanne shook her head. "That's a good start but I'm sure Mom and Dad will have him pimped out for something else soon, especially if the *Timbuktu* revival doesn't work out. No doubt they'll be willing to take whatever comes along whether it's good for Tristan or not. Hmm. I'm going to think on this."

An hour later, Portia complained, "My head hurts."

"Mine, too." Roxanne had come up with nothing. She had too much on her mind. "Being diabolical takes time. We have to think about how to get him to grow up and pursue his real dream."

Portia simply sighed and rubbed her temples.

"I'm going to have to put this aside. Nick is coming

over and we're going over some of the new information I found about his mother's family."

"Then I'm out of here." Portia jumped to her feet and grabbed her purse. She kissed Roxanne on the cheek. "I'll see you tomorrow."

The doorbell rang. Roxanne opened the door and Nick smiled at her.

"Did you uncover any more family secrets?" He stepped into the hallway and brushed rain from his hair. Summer was usually hot and dry, but an unexpected thunderstorm had swept through and drenched the city.

Roxanne grinned. "I found your grandfather Lionel Stanton." She ushered him into the dining room where her charts and laptop covered the table almost completely.

"You mean he's still alive." Nick was stunned.

"Very much so and he lives in Pasadena."

Nick stared at her. She rummaged through the pile of papers on the table. She held out a newspaper article about the Jet Propulsion Laboratory managed by Caltech and the name Lionel Stanton. The headline stated Scientist Develops Cleaner Airplane Engine.

He took the article eagerly and scanned it. "I wonder if my mother has ever been in touch with him."

Roxanne shook her head. "That isn't something I'd be able to find. You'd have to ask her."

Nick set the article down. "I never expected this."

"Like I said, family secrets come out. And I still have a long way to go. Lionel was born in New York." She pointed at two names on the chart. "Lionel's father, James

Stanton, played the saxophone at The Cotton Club." She handed him another article along with a birth certificate for Lionel with his parents' names on it—James William Stanton and Elizabeth Hart. The second newspaper article contained information about The Cotton Club and the newest band leader, saxophonist James Stanton and his Merry Vagabonds. A blurry photo of a man in a white jacket and black pants completed the article.

"This is amazing." Nick read the article. "Who knew my mother's love of music came from her own grandfather." A grandfather and a great-grandfather he didn't even know existed until this moment. He felt a small thrill of excitement yet at the same he didn't understand why his mother had kept this a secret.

"Do you think she knows that?"

"I don't know." She had to know. She had a passport which meant a birth certificate had to be produced to prove citizenship. But the idea of meeting his biological grandfather so he could ask took root in his mind. "I want to meet this man."

"I figured you might. You're not going to yell at an old man are you? He's eighty-three. I don't want to give him a heart attack."

"I'm not going to yell at an old man. I just want to know why he's not a part of our lives."

"Sometimes not having family be a part of your life isn't a bad thing," Roxanne said wryly.

"I understand what you mean, but this isn't the same thing."

"I realize that. If this guy turns into a real jerk, don't blame me."

"Duly noted," Nick said. "Let's go. Right now."

Roxanne looked surprised. "Do you want me to be part of this?"

"You already are." He glanced at his watch, calculating the time needed to get to Pasadena in the middle of the afternoon. "If we leave now, we should get there in about an hour."

"Shouldn't you talk to your mother before you do anything? He is her father. Besides, there's no guarantee he'll be home or even want to see you." Roxanne frowned.

"I want to meet this man first and then I'll talk to my mom." Roxanne may be right, but this man might be the kind of man his mother needed to be protected from. After all, why would his grandmother keep him a secret after all these years?

"All right. Let's go. But do let me give you a preemptive 'I told you so.'"

"Okay."

Roxanne grabbed her purse and her MacBook along with the articles and a couple blank charts.

Nick drove while Roxanne fed him directions from her iPhone. The freeway was crowded, but the rain had abated.

Lionel Stanton lived on a street shaded by giant live oaks and flowering magnolias. Nick parked in front of a small Craftsman bungalow that looked like it had been built in the 1930s. A broad veranda stretched across the front of the house and down one side. White wicker chairs sat on either side of an arched door, with hanging plants spaced along the front of the veranda.

Nick parked in front of the house trying to still his nerves. A rain-drenched magnolia shaded the veranda on one side. Colorful summer flowers lined the edges of the property and the brick sidewalk leading to the veranda. A white Toyota Camry sat in the driveway.

"You can still back out." Roxanne turned off her phone and put it back in her purse. "Nobody knows you're here and won't judge you if you don't see him."

"I should be courageous enough to do this."

"The unknown is difficult," Roxanne said.

"I want to do this," Nick said stubbornly as he got out of his car. He stood staring up at the house. The unknown waited and he wondered if he was opening a can of worms or finding the golden ring.

Roxanne joined him on the sidewalk.

Nick decided he would gain nothing if he didn't move forward. He strode up the brick walkway and onto the veranda. Before he could press the doorbell, the door opened and an elderly man stood in the shadow.

The man stood around five eight or nine. Snow-white hair contrasted against his deeply lined face. He stood erect with shoulders straight and head held high.

"I wondered," the man said as he stepped and ushered them into the house, "how long it would take one of you to start looking for me."

"Excuse me," Nick said.

"You look a lot like me when I was your age. Come on in."

Roxanne followed Nick into the house and into the large living room.

"That's a two-way street," Nick said. "You knew where we were." He felt a small touch of anger. This man was his biological grandfather and he knew where his grandchildren were.

Lionel Stanton sat down heavily in a recliner. "I did. Divorce was a big taboo in the 1950s and your grandmother didn't want people knowing about our failed marriage. So I agreed to stay away. But that didn't mean that I didn't love your mother, or even you."

Nick stared at him stunned. Divorce was so common now, he had a hard time understanding that at one time it hadn't been.

Roxanne held out her hand. "Hello, Mr. Stanton. I'm Roxanne."

"I recognized you from *Celebrity Dance*."

Roxanne smiled at him. "Nick hired me to do a genealogy of his mother and I'm afraid your position on the family tree was revealed quite unexpectedly."

"Every family has secrets."

"And you're one of them," Nick said.

"Are you going to tell your mother that you found me?"

"Eventually." Nick didn't quite know how to feel. He worried he would be hurting his mother's feelings by finding her father, but at the same time, he wanted to know. "What happened?"

Lionel sighed. "We were too young and your grandmother hated military life, the constant moving, always having to find new friends. Officers' wives were expected to act a certain way. And they were always under scrutiny by higher-ranked wives. One wrong move could destroy an officer's career. The stress was just too much for your grandmother."

Nick couldn't calm down. He found himself wandering the living room. The walls were decorated with photos of Lionel and other officers. The early photos showed mostly other black officers, but as the years passed, the photos contained more white officers.

A woman entered the living room. She was a tiny woman with a round body and cloud of white hair that framed an elegant face. "Lionel. I see you have company."

"This is my grandson Nick." Lionel's smile was tight and stressed. "And his friend Roxanne. This is my wife, Molly."

If Molly was surprised, she never showed it. Molly gave Nick and Roxanne a cheerful smile and graciously said, "I was just about to make tea. Would you like some?"

Nick nodded.

Roxanne jumped to her feet. "I'll help."

With Roxanne and Molly gone, the tension in the air increased.

"I realize I'm a bit presumptuous dropping in like this, but until this morning, I didn't even know you were still alive."

Lionel smiled. "My old heart can still take a surprise or two."

"Does my mother know that you live here?" Grace Torres had never once hinted that Grandpa Al was her stepfather or that she had a biological father who wasn't a part of her life.

"I don't think so." Lionel looked sad. "We've never been in contact. Her stepfather was a good man and your mom was happy with him. My being in her life would have been awkward. Like I said, it was a different time, then, and divorces were handled a bit differently. Sometimes, it's just easier to let things alone. I had to respect your grandmother's wishes. I do want you know I didn't neglect her. I paid for her support and set up a trust fund to help her through college. I followed her career and sometimes I would dream of telling her how proud I was of everything she'd accomplished."

Nick's emotions were in turmoil and he couldn't make heads or tails of them. He gazed at Lionel and saw little things in the man's face that reminded him of his mother. Her eyes were the same shape and her mouth had the same tiny upward tilt at the corners.

"So you married Molly."

"We've been married almost thirty years. No children, though." Lionel's voice was filled with regret.

Nick wondered how to proceed from here. He wasn't certain how to tell his mother. And contacting Lionel Stanton somehow seemed like a betrayal of his mother's trust. He'd stepped into an awkward situation and had made it even more awkward. And what was Nick going to tell his siblings? *Hey, guys, guess what I found out about our mother.*

"What do you want to do?" Nick asked.

"I'd like to touch base with your mom and all my grandchildren, but I don't want to make things difficult."

Difficult was an understatement.

Molly and Roxanne returned. Molly carried a plate of

cookies and Roxanne held a tray with a teapot and mugs on it. She set the tray on the coffee table and stepped back with a quizzical look at Nick.

"I don't know what to say," Nick finally said, "I need to talk to my mother."

Lionel nodded. "I'll abide by any decision you make, but I do want to say, I would very much like a relationship with all of you. I've been wanting to make things right for a long time."

Molly glanced at her husband. She patted his arm, a gentle look on her face.

Roxanne poured the tea. Nick didn't know what to do now that the knowledge was out in the open. At least for him.

He tried for small talk with Lionel, but the situation became even more awkward. Finally Roxanne suggested they leave and let all the information that had just come to light be processed.

Nick gave Lionel his phone number. And Molly smiled sweetly at him as she opened the front door and let them out.

Back in the car, Nick studied the house for a moment.

"What do you want to do?"

"I don't want to be alone."

"Let's go back to my house." She tugged on his arm and he followed her to the car still unsure how he was supposed to feel.

Roxanne opened her front door. She called out to see if her grandmother was home, but Donna didn't answer. She put her purse on the hall table and found a note from her grandmother saying she was dining with friends and would be back late.

"First," she said, "dinner. I'm starving and you need time to process everything."

In the kitchen, she put a bottle of wine in the fridge to chill and forced Nick to sit down at the snack bar. He seemed a little lost and she hurt for him. "Family is always full of surprises."

"That was a lot to handle," he said.

"That's a lot for anyone to handle," she said as she rummaged through the freezer to see if Donna had any leftovers she could use. She found some stew and frozen garlic bread. She set the stew in the microwave to defrost and leaned against the counter watching Nick. He sat at the snack bar, elbows on the surface propping his head up. He looked like a lost, vulnerable little boy. She ached to comfort him.

He said little as they ate. Afterward, they sat on the patio swing watching the sun go down over the ocean.

She didn't remember who kissed whom first. Just that his lips were on hers and the heat of his body sent her blood racing through her veins. She gasped. His kiss deepened and she suddenly pushed back and stood.

"I don't think we should give the neighbors a show," she said. She held out her hand and led him into the house and straight to her bedroom.

Warmth rose off his skin. He smelled like cool water and man. She bit her bottom lip realizing she was lost. She let her gaze explore him from his wide shoulders down to his narrow waist. She wanted him so badly.

Desire rose inside her and should have scared her,

but didn't. He made her feel safe, protected, but mostly wanted. Very much wanted. That sensation hadn't happened to her in a long time. Her stomach somersaulted as he moved closer. She closed her eyes for a second and imagined his hands on her body, his lips on hers and him inside her. Nick was her every fantasy come to life.

He shrugged. "Roxanne. Tell me you want me." She tilted her head. "I do."

He brushed a strand of hair off her cheek, answering her with a seductive smile. The tip of his finger left a trail of fire on her skin. "Good."

Roxanne prayed she wouldn't embarrass herself. Her nerves were doing the funky chicken about now. She hadn't been with someone in a long time, but the burning desire in his brown eyes gave her confidence.

Heat spiraled out of control and she felt his hands grip the hem of her shirt and pull it off. She unhooked her bra and bared herself to him.

He smiled and stared into her eyes. "We can go slow." He ran his finger along her chin and then down her throat.

"Slow is good."

"Slow it is." He kissed her neck. He licked the hollow of her throat at the pulse that she was sure he could feel jumping.

Roxanne felt his tongue against her skin. She reached up and slipped her arms around his neck.

"You taste good." He nibbled the spot where her shoulder connected with her neck.

She moaned. Heat engulfed, spinning outward from her core.

"Slow is real good." He licked her lower lip.

Who was she kidding? She didn't want slow. She wanted everything he had to give.

"I want you." Nick grabbed her wrist and guided her hand to the bulge in his jeans. He was so hard, the material of his jeans seemed to barely contain him. Roxanne gave him a squeeze, liking how he felt in her hand.

Nick slid his hand over her stomach. His warm fingers teased her skin. She held her breath.

The velvet texture of his skin consumed her.

He eased his fingers up her stomach, until he touched the curve of her breast. He moved with a deliberate intensity. She enjoyed his touch. She let her head loll back.

Her whole body trembled as she leaned toward him, and he fondled her breast. Her nipples beaded to hard points.

Nick drew in a harsh breath.

Her lips parted and Nick kissed her. She responded, her tongue touching his.

She fit her body closer to him, molding against him. "Maybe slow is overrated."

"Maybe." He pulled back a bit and laughed and slipped his hands around her.

He ran his tongue down her neck to the tops of her breasts, then to her nipples and back to her mouth. "I want you."

Roxanne moaned as she rubbed herself against him.

"You are so beautiful."

Funny, when most men said that to her, she couldn't care less, but from him it sounded so right. She liked how he made her feel. She unbuttoned his shirt to reveal his hard chest. Then she freed the buttons of his jeans and reached inside to grasp him, giving him a gentle squeeze.

"Slow is for losers." He leaned over and kissed her again. He sank his fingers into her hair and pulled her head back, exposing her throat to plant a kiss on her neck. "You taste good."

"Make love to me."

He pushed her pants and underwear down and slid his fingers inside her. Her muscles contracted under his touch. She groaned.

"I plan to." Before he slipped out of his jeans, he grabbed a condom from his pocket. He ripped the packet off and slid on the condom.

Somehow they ended up on her bed, the sheets cool beneath her heated skin. For a few moments time stood still as he entered and moved deep inside her.

She could feel her orgasm building. Spurred by the intense sensation, she wrapped her legs around him, feeling his taut muscles work under her legs. A low moan escaped her mouth. She was almost there. Thrusting her hips up, she took him all the way inside her. Her body rushed toward that peak. Her muscles clenched around him.

He began to thrust harder.

Roxanne couldn't breathe. She was almost over the edge. He buried himself inside her, pumping hard. She pushed her hips against him and spasmed in release.

Chapter 8

"Don't you think this dance is a bit simple?" Roxanne asked. She felt awkward as she stood in the center of the rehearsal studio watching him explain the steps. After their night of love making, she didn't know how to act with him. A cameraman filmed their rehearsal and she wondered if their night of passion showed on her face.

Nick had chosen the iconic meeting between Dorothy and the Scarecrow from *The Wizard of Oz*.

"Not simple," Nick said. "Effortless." He positioned her and then took up his own stance. The music started and she twirled around him while he acted as though he truly was made of straw.

She stumbled and he just grinned. "Again."

She started from the beginning, but keeping her mind on the dance was difficult after last night. The memory of his hands on her body sent spirals of heat through her. And now as they moved through the dance steps she couldn't box up the memory so she could keep her mind on her steps.

They moved through the routine a couple more times. The cameraman, having gotten what he wanted for the show, waved as he took off, leaving them to finish in private.

"You're getting better," Nick said.

"I'm just getting better at moving my feet faster and catching myself before I fall."

Nick laughed. He whirled her around. The preshow interview had been that morning and Roxanne realized she was beginning to relax.

Nick kissed the tip of her nose. "Keep your mind on the steps."

"Hard to after last night."

"I am kind of impressed with myself."

Roxanne punched his shoulder. "Stop that."

"The whole world knows we kissed."

"I don't want the whole world to know we've gone way beyond the kiss." Roxanne's body tingled at the memory of him in her bed, his solid warmth and gentle lovemaking. Even though she'd dated over the years, she hadn't found a man she could tolerate long enough to get beyond the getting-to-know-you stage. She always had the feeling that her parents had set her up with some of the men she'd gone out with. Too often the men would question her about her relationship with her parents and once the word *parent* was out of his mouth she was gone. She'd walked out a number of times on men who'd pushed and prodded so much she just knew her parents were trying to trap her into some outburst that they could exploit.

And now she'd allowed Nick to get close to her and worried he would leave because of the crazy that was in her life at the moment.

"You're frowning," Nick said. "Stop frowning."

"I'll try." She paused for a moment. "Not working. I'm afraid I made a mistake."

"What do you mean?"

"You've been exposed to the crazy that's my life. Do you want to get any deeper?"

"I like you. I'll deal with the crazy because I have my own brand of crazy."

"Deveraux crazy is special."

"True," Nick countered, grinning. "But I still think I'm man enough to take it."

Roxanne tilted her head. "I've never heard anything about you."

"Broadway is a long way from Hollywood."

"So what happened?"

"Her name is Margo Kirby."

"I've heard of her." Margo was one of the top-grossing Broadway performers.

"I choreographed her last show." He frowned as he slowed to a stop. "And we kind of got involved and things went downhill from there."

So I'm not the first colleague Nick has gotten involved with?

"Did you love her?"

"Looking back, I think I was in love with the idea of being in love with her."

"Did she love you?" Her words sounded stilted.

"No, she wanted to own me." He slid an arm around her and drew her into a step. They practiced a few more minutes and he stopped again. "She wanted her own personal pet and I didn't want that."

"What happened?"

"She turned nasty. And my reputation suffered. When Mike offered me a chance to relocate here, I took it."

She cupped his cheek knowing how he felt.

They twirled a bit more with Nick coaxing her to smile.

"What are you going to do about your grandfather?" she asked when they stopped to take a quick break and drink water.

"See, I have my brand of crazy, just like yours."

"I don't think finding a missing part of your family is crazy." She understood his ambivalence. How did a person react after discovering that everything they knew was something else entirely?

"I'm going to talk to my brother Daniel about how this needs to be handled. Daniel's good at making sense of difficult situations."

"You started this search for your mom and for you because you wanted to know, too, and it's not turning out the way you envisioned."

"My mother is a tough woman. She can roll with the punches and I'll be telling her the truth because she would want to know."

She took a sip from her water bottle and recapped it. “Come by tonight. My grandmother helps me and she’s uncovered a little bit more about Lionel Stanton’s ancestors. I think you’ll enjoy finding this out.”

He smiled at her in such an intimate way that her insides went all soft and rubbery. “I’ll be there. I could bring dinner.”

“Thanks, but my grandmother is on a cooking binge and my refrigerator is stuffed with food.”

Nick rang the doorbell. Roxanne opened the door and grinned at him.

“You look happy,” he said.

“I am.” She stood aside and gestured him into the house. “I found some interesting news.” She led the way to her dining room.

The house smelled deliciously of fresh bread. His mouth watered. “What kind of news?”

She pulled a sheet of paper out of a folder and handed it to him. “I discovered a little more about your grandfather Lionel. His family settled in Philadelphia in 1870. And you’ll never guess where they came from.”

“Come on, he’s black, it’s a gimme.”

She grinned and handed him another sheet of paper with a list of names. “His family migrated from England. This is the passenger list of the steamer, *Summerland*.” She pointed to a name. “Dr. Charles Stanton, his wife, Victoria Stanton, and two children, Cornelius and Miles, traveled from London to New York.”

He studied the list. “So my grandfather’s family

came from England. What's so important about that? England had slaves, too."

"Your ancestor and his family traveled first-class."

Nick took another look at the passenger manifest. "I'm not certain I know what that means."

"Your ancestors had money. A lot of money."

He squinted at the names. "First-class! I don't know what you're getting at." He tried to wrap his mind around the fact that his grandfather's family had come from England.

"You are not understanding. First class in 1870 was not the same as first class today where you might get a better seat and a warm, moist towel. First class in 1870 meant you had a butler, a maid, maybe your own personal chef and possibly a nanny for the kids. I doubt the use of *doctor* was honorary."

He frowned at the list of names realizing that his idea of where his family might have come from might not have been correct. "So where do you go from here?"

"I have contacts in England and though it will take some time, I think this trail is going to go somewhere unexpected. And since my grandmother provides cheap labor…"

"I heard that," a voice called from the second floor.

"…and is incredibly nosy, we're going to give her a day or two to search through English records."

"What kind of records?"

"First off," she said with a smile, "we know he was a doctor. So that means medical school. Since he had enough money for first-class tickets for himself and his family that meant he probably attended a good school. Edinburgh is where we'll start and branch off from there."

"Charles Darwin and Sir Arthur Conan Doyle went there."

She grinned and handed him another sheet of paper which appeared to be a newspaper article. As he read, he felt a deep surge of excitement.

> The Right Honorable Lord Baron William Bartlett of Kindersley House, Sussex, announces the engagement of his daughter, the Honorable Victoria Bartlett, to Dr. Charles Stanton, a London physician.

"Wow," he said.

"Your three-times great-grandmother came from minor aristocracy."

He read the marriage announcement again. "I don't know what to say."

"In the world as we know it, there isn't much that trumps English nobility."

"How is that possible? They were black."

"England was a different country."

"But England did have slaves."

She nodded. "But not all blacks were slaves. From what little research I've done so far, blacks started appearing in England in the mid-1500s. That doesn't mean they didn't have as tough a time in England as they did in America, but in order to get a better picture, I need to do more research. One thing I will say about the English—they were masters at record keeping. Not as good as the Germans, but pretty close."

"I'm stunned."

"Like I told you up front, looking for your ancestors is going to dig up a lot of information and a lot of secrets and a lot of gaps."

"Is there a way to find out why Dr. Stanton left England?"

"That's my grandmother's job. She hasn't found anything yet and tomorrow is another day. Digging through history is an enormous jigsaw puzzle and painstakingly slow. So you need to be patient."

"I don't think my mother knows any of this."

"A lot of times, stories are handed down from generation to generation and the facts get scrambled. Imagine waking up one day and looking at yourself in the mirror and realizing you're related to Thomas Jefferson. A few months later you meet your blue-eyed, blond-haired cousin. Until DNA tests were done, no one officially knew about his distaff side even though speculation raged for years. Imagine the shock around the dining table one day. And look at me—I'm from a long line of con men. Ending up acting put me right inside the family business."

"It's a lot to take in."

"And until all the facts are found, all you have is a lot of unrelated information." Roxanne shuffled through the files on the table. "I'm going to need time before I can make a cohesive report."

"But it is exciting."

She grinned at him. "I love discovering all these little facts and putting them in order."

Donna clattered down the stairs, a small duffle bag over her shoulder. "Heading out to bingo," she said as she passed them. She kissed Roxanne on the forehead, waved at Nick and was gone, the front door slamming shut after her.

Nick wasn't totally certain how he felt. He had a friend who'd been deeply disappointed that his ancestors hadn't been slaves, but even more upset because his ancestors had owned their own slaves. History was filled with anomalies.

He needed to think about this. Everything he thought he knew about his mother's family history wasn't at all what he thought it would be.

"You want to do some more tonight?"

He looked at her and he could feel the desire tighten in his belly. "Nope."

"You should relax."

"You are right."

"Good." She kissed him.

He slipped his jacket off and let it slide to the floor before wrapping his arms around her. Then he lifted her up and he felt her wind her arms around his neck, pressing her lips against his.

After what seemed like hours he slid her down his body until her feet touched the ground. "Well, hello to me." He kissed her again. His body was aching for her. He had to have her now.

She moved against him and slid her tongue over his lower lip.

He groaned and pulled her closer to him. He couldn't seem to get enough of her. She made everything in his world seem right. He thought he'd been serious about a woman before, but Roxanne was a hurricane compared to that little afternoon breeze that meandered through his life. She was everything he didn't know he wanted until she showed up in his world.

"When you kiss me like that, I have a hard time thinking about much of anything."

"Good, I've done my job." She pulled him back down and kissed him again.

He nipped her lower lip, sending shivers of pleasure down his spine and to the rest of his body.

Roxanne slid her hand down his back slowly as if she were committing his body to her memory. She moved her hands back up and between their bodies to unbutton his shirt.

Nick pulled back to help her take off his shirt. They continued kissing as they reached the bed. Nick picked her up and placed her on the bed, keeping one leg on each side of her. He pressed his lips to her mouth as her hands explored his skin. He wished she were wearing less clothing so Nick slid his hands under the hem of her T-shirt and pulled it over her head.

He kissed a trail down her neck and somehow got her out of her lacy red bra. When he reached the tops of her breasts, he pressed his mouth to one nipple, teasing it to stiffness. He slid his finger along the waistband of her thong, kissing her jaw and moving down her neck. Nothing had ever felt so wonderful in all his life. Her skin was warm and satiny. A molten feeling spiraled through him.

She fumbled his belt off. He was anxious to get out of his pants and inside of her before he lost control. Again he helped her finish the job and kicked his pants and shoes off. His socks came next and he thanked God that his dancer's body was flexible. He stumbled off the bed, shucked his boxers and quickly got himself protected with a condom, before slipping back onto the bed.

He kissed her hard. She arched up and his hands moved to her back. He moved down to her hips, sliding his fingers into the waist of her panties and then sliding them off. He pulled back to look at her.

"You are perfect." His kiss was soft but demanding before suddenly turning deep and hard.

She giggled. "Thank you. You're not bad, yourself."

His hands were everywhere, soothing and causing a yearning in her. When he palmed one of her breasts and bent to take the firm nipple into his mouth, she gasped.

He teased the other nipple with his fingers, pinching it lightly. He kissed the space between her breasts and started moving down her stomach, occasionally nipping the soft skin as he went.

A moan escaped her lips.

His hands moved her legs apart and he slid a finger into her soft, molten core. He moved down and slid his tongue over the wet sensitive skin, and sliding into her before moving back up, teasing her. He moved his tongue over her again and again. She groaned from the pleasure and heat he brought out of her. Just when he thought she couldn't take any more, he felt her muscles tighten and release with the full power of her orgasm. He moved up and slid himself inside her, never taking his eyes off her.

For a moment he didn't move, just watching her face. She pulled him closer so that she could kiss him, moving over his face to kiss his jaw, throat and chest. When she slid her tongue over the spot where his neck met his jaw, he groaned and started moving in slow strokes with her. She pressed her hips into his, sensing his need for more of her. He took the encouragement and began moving harder and faster. His pleasure was so intense that when he slid his hand between them for a moment, finding her bud, she came almost instantly. He continued to move inside her as he teased and pinched her hardened nipples. The combination of the sensations set him on fire. He was dying trying to keep a handle on himself. Seeing her pleasure, Nick began moving faster until he let out a scream of his own. He lay down on the bed beside her and pulled her into his chest.

"That was pretty all right."

She blew out a long breath. "The dismount was a little shaky."

"I will work on that."

"Give me a minute so the stars realign."

"I can do that."

She burst out laughing. And again he was amazed how comfortable she made him feel.

"Hello," Portia said as she entered the kitchen.

Roxanne glanced over her shoulder as she stood at the stove cooking bacon. "You're here awfully early."

Portia sniffed. "What's for breakfast?"

"Omelets."

"Why are there four plates on the counter?"

"I was expecting you for breakfast," Roxanne said.

Portia frowned at her. "I didn't know I was even

going to come until half an hour ago. Mom is having a meltdown of some sort and I needed to get away."

Nick entered the kitchen, his hair damp from his shower, shirt unbuttoned and no shoes on his feet.

Portia stared at him. Roxanne resisted the urge to poke her sister.

"Hello, there," Portia said with a smug glance back at her sister. "I see the two of you have gotten to the after-kissing stage."

"Would you believe we were rehearsing and it got so late, Nick spent the night?"

"I believe that a whole lot," Portia replied, sarcasm in her tone.

"Actually," Nick said, "I'm just a figment of your imagination."

Portia punched his shoulder. "For a figment of my imagination, you take a good punch."

Nick just laughed. He sat down at the kitchen table. Roxanne opened the oven and pulled out a platter to slide an omelet onto a plate. She added bacon and set the plate in front of him.

"Are you still staying for breakfast?" Roxanne asked her sister.

"That's why I'm here." Portia sat at the table across from Nick, braced her elbows on the table and rested her chin on her interlaced fingers. "You realize this would be gold for Mom and Dad, don't you?"

"And I know you will never tell them." Roxanne slid another omelet onto a plate, added bacon and placed the plate in front of her sister.

"Not in a million years, but you need to know that our parents hired a private investigator to spy on you."

Roxanne stared at her sister. "You're kidding." Would this person be dogging her every step? She and Nick would have to be more circumspect.

"I never kid about things like that." Portia popped a bit of bacon into her mouth.

Their grandmother entered the kitchen and, after a sharp look at Portia, added an extra mug to the table and started pouring coffee. She studied Nick for a second, a knowing look in her eyes before filling his mug, as well.

"Do you know who they hired?" Donna asked. She frowned as she sat down.

"Not yet, but I'll find out." Portia took a sip of coffee.

"This is not good." Roxanne filled a plate for her grandmother and set about making another omelet for herself. Then she sat down next to Nick. "What am I going to do? I'm a grown woman and they want to control me…again."

Donna patted Roxanne's hand. "Just ignore them."

"If I react, I send the wrong message. If I don't react, I send the wrong message." Roxanne rubbed her temples. Her parents could take any reaction from her and change it to make them look good and make her look like the most vile villain in the world. "How did our family turn out to be so dysfunctional?"

Portia chuckled. "Dysfunctional would be an upgrade."

"Let me deal with them," Nick said. "What can they say about me? If they indulge in a petty squabble with me, they look bad. I may have only been in Los Angeles a few years, but I'm not without my resources."

Roxanne didn't know if she was comforted or not. On

one hand she felt protected by Nick's announcement, but on the other hand she felt as though she should solve her own problems.

Nick finished his breakfast, cleared his plate and coffee mug from the table and loaded them in the dishwasher.

"Sometimes," Donna said, "I regret not fighting harder to keep Eli when Rasheed and I divorced. But I wanted Eli to know his father, I just didn't think Eli would turn out so vindictive."

Roxanne held up a hand. "Stop, Grandma, our father turned out the way he turned out because of his decisions. He had choices. He ran things with whatever was the least amount of work. He put his children to work supporting him. What does that say about him?" Or her mother who followed right along with those decisions.

Donna shrugged.

"I have to get going, I have a meeting in forty minutes. Let me handle things for you, Roxanne. I'll see you at the dress rehearsal at ten." He bent over to kiss her cheek, grinned at Donna and Portia and left.

A few minutes later, Roxanne heard the sound of his car starting up and fading away.

"I need to shower and get ready for the fitting." Roxanne pushed away from the table. "The first elimination round is tomorrow night and I want to be ready." Hopefully she would be, but right now her heart wasn't in it.

Nick stood in the waiting area. Outside, the band was tuning up. Roxanne stood next to him bouncing back and forth on her toes.

"Calm down," he said.

"I'm too nervous," she replied. "If I don't do well, I'll be gone."

"No, you won't," he said. "You've improved and social media is solidly in your corner." He slid an arm around her. She looked fabulous in her cute little Dorothy outfit, though it was a lot more seductive than the original movie costume. Small red hearts dotted both the blue skirt and the crop top. The skirt came to midthigh and the crop top revealed her toned abs. White fishnet stockings adorned her legs to just over her knees contrasting with the red sparkly dance shoes on her feet. Her hair was braided and the plaits hung down to her shoulders.

Nick's own costume itched. Someone had the bright idea to use real straw to simulate the scarecrow's outfit. Straw poked out of his hat and the neck of his plaid shirt. The shirt was torn and a few pieces of glued-on straw decorated the holes. The bottom of the pants ended midcalf and large red hearts decorated the legs.

"You look pretty sexy," Roxanne said.

"For the first time in my life, I understand that beauty is painful."

She frowned. "What do you mean?"

"I may look hot on the outside, but the inside of my pants itches."

"I'm lost here." Roxanne glanced up and down.

"Somebody had the bright idea to glue straw on the insides of my pants." He gestured at the wisps of straw hanging from his pockets. "I will not be unhappy to lose this costume when the evening is over."

"If you're nice to me, I'll happily help you scratch your itch." She gave him a coy smile.

"I'm going to let you, sexy Dorothy."

The director finally had the cameras in position. The opening dancers stood on their spots and the band opened with their first number. The audience stilled, all eyes on the dance floor. The opening dance number began. Credits rolled across the monitor as the show got under way.

Their dance went a lot smoother than their first one. Roxanne was more comfortable and Nick felt a spurt of pride as she moved almost gracefully into each step. The judges were kind.

"I'm surprised I didn't get eliminated," Roxanne said.

Nick walked her to her car. "The audience loves you."

"I feel a little sorry for Barbie. I thought she did well."

Nick shrugged. Barbie Foster had been a model whose wild lifestyle had derailed her career and she was now trying for a comeback.

"The audience liked her well enough, but they loved you more," Nick replied.

She clicked her remote at her car. A tiny beep sounded and the interior lights came on.

"But she did well. It seems as though the competition has nothing to do with talent, but popularity."

"That will end after a few more eliminations and it gets harder to decide. Right now everyone is still in the beginner phase. With the exception of Norma Dover, everyone else started at the same place."

Norma was an Olympic ice-skater and dancing was a normal part of her routine.

Nick opened the door to the driver's side for her.

"Later on," he continued, "the decisions the judges

will make will be based on improvement rather than ability. Today, you were more comfortable on the dance floor. For the first time your normal bubbly self was as much a part of your dance as you were."

Roxanne looked pleased. "I'll have to practice harder."

"You need to practice bringing more of yourself onto the dance floor. Kirstie Alley was hilarious on *Dancing With the Stars*. The audience loved her and even though she didn't win, she made it to the final round and most of that was because of her personality."

"I'm hardly in her league," Roxanne said.

"Last season, Mia Gallier stated up front she was overweight and over-the-hill and she still won. And trust me, I have the broken toes to prove it."

She gave him a sharp glance. "What are you saying?"

"Mia was a terrible dancer for the first six weeks and then something just clicked with her. From the first episode she was the fan favorite. She had this wonderful biting wit and was hilariously self-deprecating. The audience had a hard time not falling in love with her. If she hadn't won, I think riots would have happened."

He wanted to kiss her, but was conscious of the possibility of a hidden camera trained on them. "Tomorrow we're taking the day off."

"And doing what?" She tilted her head up at him, a soft smile on her face.

"We're having a day at the beach. Mike and Nancy have invited us for lunch. They have their own slice of beach and we can relax."

"Sounds delightful, but I do have work to do on your genealogy."

"You said you were waiting for information from England and it would take a few days. I'm not a task-master. I think you can take a day off."

She eyed him speculatively as though weighing his words. "I guess I can take a day."

She opened the door to her car, got in and started the motor. She waved as she backed out of the parking space and headed to the street.

Nick watched her go, wishing he were going with her, but he was having a late dinner with his parents at their restaurant. Once a month was standard procedure for the whole family to get together after the restaurant closed at eleven. They would cook and talk and just be a family.

How he would get through it knowing the truth about his mother's father was beyond him.

What was he going to do? He knew he needed to talk to her, but he didn't have the words just yet and everything needed to be just right.

Roxanne practically waltzed into the house on winged feet to find her grandmother and Portia waiting for her.

"You did good tonight," her grandmother said.

"I was third from the bottom."

"No," Donna said, "you were being cunning and letting everyone else be overconfident."

"Yes, Grandma, let's go with that." Roxanne filled a glass with ice and water and drank it down in one gulp.

"I think you did wonderfully," Portia said.

"I feel better about my performance and I feel that I've improved. Also, I didn't see Mom and Dad. If they were there they were keeping themselves on the down low." Just knowing her mother wouldn't be able to criticize her to her face made her happy.

Portia grinned. "We were having a family meeting."

Instantly, Roxanne was filled with dread and suspicion. "What did we meet about?"

"Strategy," Portia said. "Mom and Dad are trying to figure out a way to blackmail you so you'll do the movie."

"Good luck with that." Roxanne refilled her glass of water and drank a second one. Since she'd started dancing with Nick, she drank a ton more water than she normally did.

"The private eye isn't getting much on you. You lead an incredibly boring life, sister." Portia's eyes twinkled with merriment. She sipped her wine.

"Thank you."

"That poor guy talked to every one of your neighbors he could track down. They all love you. Mom and Dad were so annoyed, they fired him."

"My neighbors don't love me," Roxanne objected wondering how the private detective was able to get past the guard at the gate. "They love Grandma's oatmeal-raisin-white-chocolate-chip cookies." Donna had been wooing the neighbors since they'd first moved in. First with cookies, then handmade Christmas gifts that she hand delivered to everyone in the cul-de-sac. Donna had always been generous.

"I make the best," Donna said. "I think I need to get another couple batches out now and distribute more so everyone remembers their lines."

"Have you been bribing people again?" Roxanne asked.

"*Bribe* is such an ugly word," Donna said with as innocent a look on her face as she could manage.

"Grandma, you're the best." Roxanne kissed her grandmother, thankful the woman was on her side.

"I hid a few. Let's get a bottle of wine and eat them." Donna opened a cabinet and pulled out a cookie tin.

"I'll get the wine," Portia said and opened the wine fridge for a bottle of pinot grigio.

Roxanne grabbed three dessert plates and set them on the kitchen table. "What else happened at the meeting?"

Portia removed the cork and grabbed three wineglasses. She poured and handed a glass to Roxanne. "Mom has been talking to TMZ. They loved the video of you and Nick kissing even though they didn't get the mileage out of it they thought they would."

"And," Portia continued, "they decided that Mom would do a critical analysis of your dancing after every episode in an attempt to keep the fire going because she thinks the judges are being too kind to you."

"How does Mom think her critical comments are going to embarrass me enough to want to do the movie? They're just going to make it look like she's trying to sabotage me if the public knows the comments are hers."

"She says she has more juicy stuff that she's been saving."

"The PI just told her I have a boring life. And other than sleeping with Nick, my neighbors aren't talking."

"We have loyal neighbors and if they want more of my cookies, they know what not to say," Donna put in with a smug smile. "Besides, people don't live in this neighborhood to have their dirty laundry aired. They know better than to invite gossip into this area. If they start selling you out, you have license to do the same."

But Roxanne was still focused on her mother's plan to sell dirt on her. "I'm a grown woman. I can't imagine what she thinks she has over me."

"TMZ isn't always about what's true."

"In my opinion they are just one step away from stalking." Her mother was trying to make a mountain out of a molehill.

"Look," Portia said gently, "Mom's comments could work against her. The audience loves you and anything she says could be construed as sour grapes. All she can really offer is innuendo."

Roxanne sighed and rubbed her temples. Crap like this was one of the reasons she preferred to stay out of the spotlight.

Dread coursed through Roxanne. "A person can make a lot out of innuendo." This hostility with her parents was going to get vicious. "How do I counteract it?"

"No matter what you do they will find a way to use it. Continue ignoring them. You'll get through this."

Roxanne bit into a cookie savoring the sweet, almost spicy taste. Her grandmother added a secret ingredient which she refused to indulge. Roxanne never pushed her. Everyone was allowed secrets even if the secret was one simple ingredient to a recipe.

Secrets could destroy a family or make it stronger. She wasn't going to knuckle under to her parents' blackmail. Like her sister, she would get through this.

Chapter 9

Mike and Nancy lived in a gated community right on the beach that honored the privacy of the owners. Nick pulled in to the driveway of a two-story home painted white with gray trim.

Roxanne had never been to Nancy's home. They'd always met at a restaurant or Roxanne's home. "What a lovely place."

"Yeah, makes my condo look like it should be condemned."

Roxanne laughed. "This is what happens when old-Hollywood money marries old-Hollywood money."

"They have homes all over the world."

"Are we being jealous?" Roxanne teased.

"No. No, really. Well, maybe. Yes," Nick finally admitted.

Nick parked in the driveway. Roxanne got out of the car, realizing that Mike and Nancy's life was what her parents aspired to. Roxanne was comfortable. She would never want for anything in her life. But this was wealth with a capital *W*. These people wrote her checks. She was pleased that she and Nancy were friends. They'd been friends for a long time and in Hollywood who a person knew was more important than what a person knew. Roxanne was lucky in that she had a bankable skill, not only as an actress, but as a genealogist. And being on the crest of that popularity created new opportunities for her. Many of her contemporaries, whose careers went sideways, never recovered.

The front door swung open as they approached. A man in a black suit smiled at them.

"Good morning, Miss Deveraux, Mr. Torres. I'm Silas, Mr. and Mrs. Bertram's butler. Please come in."

Roxanne smiled at Silas. "Mr. and Mrs. Bertram are expecting us."

"I know, miss. Mr. and Mrs. Bertram will not be able to be here today. They have made the house available to you both."

"What," Nick said. "I thought…"

Silas smoothly interrupted. "They ask your forgiveness, but a small emergency required their presence." He moved aside and gestured them into the house.

Roxanne laughed. She nudged Nick. "Thank you, Silas." Nancy was an unrepentant romantic. She and her husband were matchmaking.

The house was as white inside as outside—white walls, white furniture, white marble and white carpeting. Roxanne was afraid to touch anything for fear of leaving a smudge.

"Lunch is being served on the back veranda." Silas led the way down a long hallway that bisected the house. The living room and formal dining room were on the left, and an office and a family room were on the right. In the foyer, stairs curled up to the second story. A huge country kitchen spanned the house from side to side, with a long bank of windows overlooking the ocean and a huge redwood deck. Steps led from the deck down to the beach. On the sand near the water, two lounge chairs, shaded by a large white umbrella, resided.

A woman stood in the kitchen arranging food on two plates. She nodded pleasantly at Nick and Roxanne.

Silas sat them at the table and poured lemonade into tall frosted glasses. A warm breeze brushed over Roxanne's skin as she sat and luxuriated in the calm beauty of the Pacific Ocean.

"I wasn't expecting this," Nick said.

"I'm not surprised." Roxanne hadn't expected to have the house to themselves, either, but she knew Nancy. "This is going to be a perfect day," Roxanne said.

Silas brought out two salad plates and served Roxanne and Nick with a flourish. He silently withdrew.

"I love the beach," Nick said. "The surf looks good and I know Mike has boards in the guesthouse. He surfs when he has the time."

"Surf? You surf?"

"Of course. Who doesn't?"

"I don't."

He eyed her in surprise. "Why not?"

"I enjoy the idea of the beach and surfing, but once you're in the water, you become part of the food chain. Didn't you see the photo on the internet of the woman with her two children frolicking in the surf and the ten-foot shark outlined in the wave behind them?"

Nick sipped his lemonade. "I saw that, but I never believe what I see on the internet. For all you know it could have been Photoshopped."

Roxanne shrugged. "If you say so. But I don't believe you."

"Come on, I'll teach you to surf. Trust me, you'll love it."

"Really. What if I get injured?" *Or eaten by a shark.* She glanced doubtfully at the water.

"It's a mild day and these baby waves are the best waves to learn on, and I'm not going to let anything happen to you. We'll take it easy and stay close to shore."

Food chain, she chanted to herself. But pleasing Nick was important, too. "Life is about learning new things. I'll give it a try."

He grinned at her. "I knew you would."

She finished her salad. Silas whisked her plate away and refilled her lemonade.

"How are things going with your family?" Nick asked after Silas left the main course in front of them. "They've been kind of quiet the last week."

The plate consisted of a delicate white fish with a buttery-looking sauce, thin asparagus spears wrapped in an orange peel and a fluffy crescent roll.

"I think they're gathering their flying monkeys," Roxanne said wryly. "You know Portia told me they hired a private investigator to find deep, dark dirt on me, but the PI has come up empty. I'm a good neighbor, I sometimes help out at the zoo with my sister and provide a home for my grandmother. Hard to find dirt on those activities."

"Your sister is cute. I really like her."

"I know. She's trying to find a way to get to veterinary school."

"And your brother?" Nick asked.

She paused, thinking about what Portia had revealed about Tristan. "At one time, he wanted to be an environmental engineer, but I think fame has seduced him. He seems more interested in the trappings of celebrity now." The more times she saw Tristan's name in the tabloids, the more worried about him she became. "I'm worried he's about to self-destruct."

Nick nodded in understanding. "I've been avoiding him."

"He wants you to cast him as the lead in the revival of *Timbuktu*."

"I know, but it's too early. Mike and I are only in the planning stages and we're months away from casting."

"How did your parents keep you and your siblings grounded?"

"Family always comes first. We have monthly dinners and even if you live in another state, we Skype. Excuses are not allowed."

Roxanne thought about that as she ate her fish. It was delicious even though she wasn't big on fish. Silence fell, punctuated by the roar of the waves as they pounded against the sand. The rhythmic sound made her sleepy. She might not trust the ocean and its uncharted depths, but the sound always relaxed her.

After lunch, they changed in the guesthouse into bathing suits. Roxanne's one-piece bathing suit was a deep purple with white trim. Nick looked at her approvingly, though she thought she saw a slight disappointment in his eyes.

A rack of several surfboards were stored in a shed on the shady side of the guest house. Nick took one, removed it from its board bag and checked it over, smiling. "Ready?" He took her hand and headed toward the water.

"Don't you have to do something to them?" She eyed the surfboard suspiciously.

"Mike keeps them in excellent condition."

Roxanne hesitated trying to keep her calm. What were the chances of being eaten by a great white? A million to one. Five to one. She took a step and then forced herself to take another. Foaming water surged toward her.

You can do this, she told herself, hesitating as the surf surged toward her feet.

Nick waded into the water, pulling her with him. "Come on, I'm not going to let anything happen to you."

The water was cool against the intense heat. She dug her toes into the sand and allowed Nick to pull her deeper into the water. He showed her how to sit on the board. She straddled it and he sat behind her, showing her how to paddle.

Roxanne didn't expect to enjoy surfing. The waves were higher than she was comfortable with, but with

Nick's help she managed to catch a couple. She spent more time falling off the board than staying on.

"I don't think I'm ever going to be a surfer girl," Roxanne said with a laugh. She half stumbled across the wet sand after she exited the water.

"You're a native Californian, how can you not?" He sat on the surfboard watching her, appreciation in his eyes.

She simply shook her head. "I'm done. You play. Silas set up those lounge chairs for us and I'm going to enjoy them while I'm watching you."

She retreated back to the beach while Nick spent another hour on the board, paddling farther out to catch the higher waves.

While he surfed, she watched him. His body glistened with water highlighting every muscle. He was easy to look at. Farther out on the water, seagulls glided and dipped down, skimming the water, adding their raucous cries to the sound of the ocean. A pelican floated on the surface. Roxanne found her eyelids growing heavy and finally drifted to sleep.

"Tomorrow it's back to rehearsal," Nick said as he pulled into her driveway and parked next to Portia's car.

Roxanne groaned. "All this relaxation made me realize I need a vacation."

"Where do you want to go? Tahiti, Bali, Venice, Rome?"

"I want to go someplace where I don't have to work." She thought about a destination for a moment. "Antarctica. The few people there are scientists and they are only temporary."

"It's cold there," Nick said.

"You don't like the cold?"

"Not that kind of bone-numbing cold. I like skiing-in-Aspen cold."

"There's history in Aspen." She hadn't been to Colorado for a couple years. She'd attended a seminar on genealogy there and loved it. If she'd had more time she might have done some skiing.

"That's as cold as I ever want to get."

"Fair enough." She opened the car door and got out. Nick followed her up the steps. "Have you talked to your mother yet about her father?"

He shook his head. "I'm having a hard time figuring out how to tell her. I'm going to try tonight. We're meeting for dinner."

He gave her one last kiss and leaned into it. She didn't want him to go.

"I'll see you tomorrow."

She nodded and opened the front door.

Nick parked in the lot adjacent to his parents' restaurant. Daniel's car was parked next to Sebastian's, but he didn't see either of his parents' cars.

He pushed into the restaurant inhaling the spicy smells from the kitchen, hearing the muted conversation and an occasional laugh.

He sat down across from Sebastian. "What are you two doing here?"

Sebastian shuffled his deck of cards and slid them across the table. “Pick one.”

Nick did so and when Sebastian asked for it back, he slid the card into the deck without looking.

“Mom and Dad are having a date night,” Daniel said, “we’re here just keeping an eye on things.”

Even though his parents trusted their general manager, they didn’t leave anything to chance. Usually Matteus, their oldest brother, who had decided on a career in law enforcement, took up restaurant duty when his parents couldn’t be here. “What happened to Matteus?” Nick asked as a waitress poured water into a glass and set it in front of him.

“Big case,” Sebastian said. He shuffled his deck, counted the cards and held up a three of clubs.

“If you say so,” Nick said.

Sebastian grinned. “You know me too well.”

“That whole deck is probably nothing but threes of clubs.”

Sebastian shrugged. He turned the deck over to show the cards. They were all threes of clubs. Nick grinned at him. Sebastian shuffled again and the cards turned back into their normal suits.

“Have a nice day with Roxanne?” Sebastian asked. “I’m wondering when I get to meet her?”

“I tried to teach her to surf. And you’ll meet her in due time.”

Sebastian slid the cards into their box and put it away inside his pants pocket.

“I liked her,” Daniel said. The waitress brought a

basket piled with an assortment of bread. He took a roll, buttered it and took a bite.

Nick liked her, too. "I was planning on talking to Mom about something tonight. I asked Roxanne to do an ancestry search for us, I thought it would be nice to know and make a great Christmas gift."

"And you found something?" Sebastian asked.

"I found a lot of things. Or rather Roxanne found a lot of things."

"Like what?" Sebastian asked.

Nick didn't know if he should tell them, but then again, why not. "We have a grandpa."

"Grandpa Al will be happy to know that." Daniel finished his roll and searched for another.

"Not Grandpa Al," Nick said, wondering how to tell his brothers about Lionel Stanton. He felt a little guilty discussing this with them before talking to his mom.

Sebastian's eyebrows rose curiously.

"Grandpa Al," Nick said, "is not our biological grandfather." There, he'd said it. He didn't realize how the heavy weight of keeping a secret had been pulling him down.

Daniel looked surprised and Sebastian looked curious.

"And," Daniel prompted, tapping the table with his index finger.

"Grandma was married before Al to a Lionel Stanton and he's Mom's biological dad."

Daniel leaned back, his mouth open in surprise.

"Wow," Daniel said. "Who knew? Who's going to tell Mom?"

Nick glanced at Daniel. "I planned to talk to her tonight, but she's not here. You're two minutes older than me and you've been holding it over me all our lives. You talk to her."

Daniel glanced at Sebastian. "You're older than us."

"I think we should let Matteus tell her. He's the oldest and he has a gun," Sebastian said.

"Mom must know. She has a passport. So she would have needed to provide her birth certificate to get it, which would have included her biological father's name." Nick frowned.

"You can change a birth certificate," Daniel said.

"You would need a court order to change the name of a biological parent and that would be difficult to obtain," Sebastian replied. At one time he'd thought about being a lawyer, but card tricks won out.

"She's never said anything." Nick wondered if there was more than just a secret at stake.

"What do you want to do?" Daniel asked.

Nick almost wished he'd never started the process, but that wasn't fair to his mother or Roxanne. "The problem is that Lionel is still alive and he lives in Pasadena and I think he wants a relationship with us."

That shocked his brothers. Daniel stared at Nick and Sebastian frowned.

"I wasn't expecting that," Daniel said. "You've met him?"

"I wanted to check him out first."

Again his brothers looked at him in surprise.

"I wasn't expecting that, either," Daniel added.

Nick fell silent. The waitress brought spinach salads and placed the plates in front of them.

"Why?" Sebastian stared hard at Nick.

Nick didn't know why. He'd thought it was a good idea at the time. "I wanted to check him out. I thought Roxanne had made a mistake, but..." His voice trailed off.

Sebastian said, "Maybe Mom didn't say anything because she didn't know he was still alive."

Nick didn't have an answer. Their mother was so open about everything, why hadn't she ever said anything about this, unless she considered the information to be unimportant.

"Maybe we could all go meet with him," Nick said.

"Do you think we should gang up on the poor old man?" Daniel asked.

"I don't know what to think, but this is bigger than just me. Mom is going to be affected, too."

"I wonder if Dad knows?" Sebastian mused.

"I want to meet this man." Daniel glanced back and forth between Nick and Sebastian. "But before we do, we need to talk to Matteus, Nina and Lola. They should be part of this process."

"I want to get a feel for him before we break this to Mom," Daniel said.

"Mom is no wilting lily," Sebastian said. "I just don't think she knows the truth."

"Let's find out the truth and then we can talk to her," Nick replied.

"Where are we going?" Roxanne asked.

The rehearsal had been a good one and Nick seemed

buoyant about something. “I have all this excess energy today.”

“I can think of a thing or two to burn it off,” she said with a coy sideways glance at him.

He grinned. “I have something else in mind.”

“Am I going to like it?”

“Yes,” he said. “Of course you are.”

She settled back against the leather car seat and watched the scenery flash by. He turned down a side street and into a large parking lot mostly empty of cars.

The banner Studio City Roller Rink hung over a double door entrance.

“You’re kidding,” she said with a wide grin. She hadn’t been roller-skating since when, high school, maybe?

“I never kid about roller-skating.”

“Do you even know if I know how to roller-skate?”

He grinned. “I talked to Portia. She said you did as a kid.” He parked the car, slid out and opened her car door with a flourish.

Afternoon heat flooded the car. Then he opened the rear passenger door and grabbed a large black metal box from the backseat.

She remembered roller-skating around the studio when she wasn’t on the set. She’d had fun. But she hadn’t been on skates in years. “Is it even open? There’s hardly any cars in the lot.”

“I rented it for the afternoon. I know how you big stars hate having the public see you fall on your tush.”

She laughed. “I rolled down a muddy hill and played dead. The public has already seen me at my worst.”

He tugged her out of the SUV. "Come on. You'll have fun."

"I don't know if I remember how."

"It's like riding a bike. You never forget." He pulled her toward the doors.

"You're planning a dance with me and you on roller skates, aren't you?"

"I'll make that decision after I see you skate."

The interior was cool. A blast of air-conditioning lifted her hair. Muted music filled the large oval rink. An attendant on skates circled the rink in step with the music. A second attendant asked her shoe size and handed her a pair of brown skates.

Nick led her to a bench and opened his case to show gleaming black leather skates. He pulled a roll of socks out of a pocket and handed them to Roxanne. "Put these on." He opened another case and added a helmet and knee and elbow pads to her pile.

"Do I get a pillow for my tush?" she asked as she took off her shoes and rolled the socks on and then Nick knelt down in front of her and laced her into her skates, then helped her with the pads.

"Why?" she asked as he fussed with her skates.

"Balance, stability and coordination," Nick said. He sat next to her and stripped off his shoes. He slid his feet into his skates and laced them up. "All those elements are a bit out of your comfort zone."

"That's an understatement."

"This is going to make dancing seem much easier." He stood and grinned at her. He held out his hand. "Come on."

Standing wasn't as easy as she remembered. The wheels were loose and slick on the tile floor. She slipped and slid her way to the rink, afraid to pick her feet up.

The attendant waited for them at the entry to the resin floor that comprised the main rink. He held out a hand to Roxanne. "Haven't done much skating lately, have you?"

"My feet seem to remember, but my knees don't," Roxanne admitted, trying not to wobble.

"Keep your feet together," the attendant said. The name *Wes* was embroidered on his shirt. He gently pulled her out onto the floor. "I'm going to help, and I won't let you fall. A few tips to keep in mind..." He rattled off instructions while Nick took a turn around the floor looking like skating was so completely natural to him, Roxanne felt a spurt of envy.

After ten minutes of patient coaching, and picking her up after a couple falls, the attendant turned her back to Nick who took her hand. The music played more loudly.

"What dances can you do on skates?" she asked after her first circuit around the rink without falling.

"Fox-trot, waltz, polka and a pretty good tango." He wrapped one arm around her waist and took the other hand and held it out. "You'll be a master in no time."

She found herself sliding in time to the music with Nick's hand clasped tightly around her waist.

"Stop thinking about your feet," he ordered. "Go with the flow."

Going with the flow became her mantra as she worked to enjoy herself. Lulled by the music and the rhythm, she leaned into him. She'd forgotten how much she loved skating. After a few turns around the rink, she found herself relaxing and laughing, melting into his arms with a sensuality that left her almost breathless.

"I feel like my feet are still skating," Roxanne said as he opened the car door. "Are you still thinking about a dance routine on skates?"

"I changed my mind," he said as he started the car.

Twilight cast a yellow glow on the landscape. The air was thick with summer heat. "I think you're going to need to feed me."

"I can manage food. How about take-out from Mario's and then..." he hesitated on the next words "...come home with me," Nick whispered into her ear. He leaned into her, his hands moving around her waist. His need for her flamed and he kissed deeply until she groaned.

She pushed away to study him. For a long moment, she said nothing and then finally nodded.

Nick lived in a condominium just off Wilshire Boulevard. He pulled up to heavy wrought iron gates, inserted his key card and slowly, the gates opened. Roxanne looked nervous.

He liked his condo. He'd kept the decorating to a minimum—bare wood floors, brown leather furniture and white walls with a few art pieces he liked.

Roxanne looked around curiously while he opened the wine fridge behind the bar and pulled out a bottle of white wine. He popped the cork, poured two glasses and opened the brown paper bag from Mario's, which they'd stopped at on the drive over. The scent of tacos, enchiladas and spicy guacamole and corn chips filled the room. He handed her a paper plate and Roxanne grabbed a taco.

"I didn't realize I was so hungry," she said between bites.

"Roller-skating can do that to you." She sat at the bar with him, eating her food and sipping the wine. All the while he was conscious of her heat, the scent of her floral perfume and the way her eyes keep glancing at him almost shyly.

"This is good," she said as she finished an enchilada.

"Not bad."

He cleaned up when they'd finished and joined her on the sofa. He pulled her into his arms and again heat flared through him.

Nick's words caressed her. "I want you." He reached out and pulled her into his embrace. He kissed her, moving his mouth over hers, and Roxanne wrapped her arms around him. Every part of her body was ablaze. Her eyes closed and she let the passion take over. It was so wonderful being out of control. She clung to him like a desperate woman. She could feel herself growing even wetter.

Nick pulled away from her and she missed his heat the instant it was gone. "Tell me you want me to."

"More than anything." Did he have any idea how sexy he looked as he shook out his hair? Her throat went dry and she couldn't take her eyes off him. He pulled off his shirt and tossed it on the floor before striking a pose. He was stripping for her. How exciting! She found herself smiling like a lovestruck fool.

"Do you like?" Nick unbuttoned his jeans and folded one side back slightly.

She stared into his chocolate eyes. "Were you in any doubt?"

He chuckled. "Good."

She felt his laugh all the way down to her toes. "Do you want me to get undressed now?"

"Slowly."

"If that's what you want."

"It is."

Roxanne unbuttoned her shirt, slid it off and then pushed her jeans down. She slipped off her underwear and stood, her panties dangling from her fingers.

Nick snatched her panties out of her hand and tossed them on the floor. "They look good on the floor." He pointed at her. "Next."

She unhooked her bra, pulled it off and let it slide through her fingers.

He grabbed her wrist and brought her hand to his very hard penis. "This is how bad I want you."

He felt so strong, so powerful. Her heart started racing. Heat gushed between her legs.

"This is why I can't wait."

Her eyes slanted over the condom packets lying on the bed. She turned her gaze back to Nick. She let her eyes roam his beautiful sculpted chest, admiring his muscles, his skin, his everything. She watched him take off his shoes and socks, and then put the condom on. Then he grabbed her around the waist and lifted her up. "Wrap your legs around me."

Roxanne did as she was commanded and he walked

them to his bed. He put his knees on the mattress and lowered her body until she was lying on her back. Without giving her any time to think, he spread her legs.

"You are so pretty down here."

She had a moment of self-consciousness and wanted to close her legs, but then he slid two thick fingers inside her. Her back arched as she accepted him inside her. Pleasure knifed through her and her toes curled. Wetness coursed through her. She was ready to explode. Then he began to massage her clitoris. The calloused pad of his thumb moved achingly slowly over her hard bud. Roxanne couldn't catch her breath.

He moved faster, harder, driving her to the point of orgasm.

"Inside me. Please."

He smiled. "Yes."

Roxanne sighed as he removed his fingers and quickly inserted the head of his penis inside her. She looked up at Nick and his face was tight with tension. He had squeezed his eyes shut and his chest was rising and falling.

"You feel so good."

Roxanne raised herself on her arms and wriggled her hips trying to get him farther inside her.

He opened his eyes. "Do you want all of me?"

She nodded her head.

He slid his arms around her waist and lifted her up until she touched his chest. The motion forced her body to impale itself on him.

A shuddering breath escaped her mouth. She felt so full. He throbbed inside her and there was a moment where she just felt so complete. She was hanging on the edge.

He smiled against her mouth. "Hang on to me. I have you."

Roxanne put her arms around his neck. She could feel him pulsing inside her. She was ready to orgasm now.

He put his hand on her butt, cupping her cheeks, and slowly he began to move her hips up and down. He filled her so completely, Roxanne was dizzy with pleasure. Her head fell back and she just let instinct take over. She clenched her muscles around him.

His fingers pressed into her skin and his lips roamed her neck and breasts. She could feel the beginnings of stubble on his chin. He whispered against her skin, but she couldn't exactly make out his words. He suddenly sucked her nipple into his mouth and she felt herself come. "Nick."

He laughed and pushed her down hard on his penis.

She spiraled out of control, and increased her tempo, wanting him to orgasm with her. He pushed up into her and she thrust down on him.

Together they found their perfect tempo and time seemed to stop. Her pleasure escalated and their mouths collided, their tongues dancing. Their bodies strained together until Roxanne came again, Nick following her seconds later.

Chapter 10

Roxanne was almost giddy with excitement. "We weren't eliminated tonight."

"I told you roller-skating would help with your balance." Nick grinned at her as they pushed through the doors to the parking lot. "You wowed the audience tonight."

She did. Roxanne almost skipped to Nick's car. Despite her earlier misgivings the results had turned out better than she expected. "I think we make a good team."

"In more ways than one," Nick said and kissed the tip of her nose.

"What is our routine for next week?" She slid into the passenger seat.

"The rumba," Nick said as he started the car and backed out of the parking space.

"That seems complicated." At least he'd decided against a dance routine on roller skates.

"No more complicated than any other dance."

She grinned as he drove up the entry ramp to the freeway. Even at night, Los Angeles was alive with movement. Cars streamed along at top speed. Lights blazed overhead. The Pacific Ocean in the distance seemed like a black hole in the darkness.

Nick turned onto her street. Roxanne frowned at her house. Lights showed in almost every window. Usually by this time at night, her grandmother was in bed and only the porch light would be on.

Portia's car was parked in front of the house. Roxanne felt a shiver of trepidation slide down her spine. Something was wrong.

Roxanne ran into the house, Nick at her heels.

Portia sat in the family room, a glass of wine in one hand. Roxanne was surprised to find Tristan present, as well. He paced back and forth in front of the fireplace. Roxanne's grandmother sat at the kitchen table with her laptop open, frowning at the screen.

"What's going on?" Roxanne asked.

Portia jumped to her feet. "Thank goodness you're here."

Tristan's gaze flickered between Nick and Roxanne.

Donna closed her laptop and swung around to face the room.

"They're going to sue you," Portia said.

"What?" Roxanne asked.

"Mom and Dad are going to sue you," Tristan said. He flopped into a chair and stared at Roxanne.

Roxanne frowned. "Why?"

Portia said. "A couple of their clients spoke with your agent."

"And what does that have to do with me?" Roxanne asked.

"Mom and Dad decided you're behind this mass defection," Tristan said.

Perplexed, she could only stare at her sister. "I haven't done anything. I can't control what their clients do."

"Don't you know you're the great and powerful Roxanne," Portia said. "According to Mom you have magical powers." Portia drained her glass and poured another one.

"Right," Roxanne said. "I'm hungry, Nick. Do you want a sandwich?"

He nodded and she went into the kitchen and pulled lunch meats and mayo out of the refrigerator. She handed him a bottle of water.

"Roxanne, you have to take this seriously," Portia cried.

"No, I don't. They're just rattling their chains. If push comes to shove, I'm the one with the money and I can keep them in court for years. If they think I'm going to wilt over the word *lawsuit*, they need to rethink their strategy." She glanced at her brother. "Why are you here?"

"Because," Tristan said, looking ashamed, "I'm the one who started Mom and Dad thinking about lawsuits when I decided I'm not renewing my contract with them, either."

"And they aren't taking it well," Roxanne said.

"It doesn't look good when your own children desert a sinking ship." Portia opened the cookie tin to see what was inside. She pulled out cookies and set them on a plate. Tristan grabbed one and took a big bite.

"You aren't deserting a sinking ship," Roxanne said, "You just decided to go in a different direction."

"But you encouraged her," Tristan said. "Mom and Dad see that as a betrayal of all they did for you."

"I just want Portia and you to be happy." Roxanne's tone was fierce and annoyed.

"Mom and Dad say you're exerting undue influence on her and me which is harming their business," Tristan replied.

"And they can sue me for this?" Roxanne asked.

"Anybody can sue anybody for pretty much anything they want."

Roxanne piled chicken and cheese on the bread. "Just because they are planning this lawsuit doesn't mean they're going to go through with it."

"They really want to sign you for this movie."

"No. Not gonna happen." Roxanne handed a sandwich to Nick. He studied her and seeing the concern in his eyes made her want to crawl into his arms and make everything go away.

"They feel you owe them," Portia said.

Roxanne frowned. "In what way?"

"When you didn't do the movie they signed you for when you were sixteen, they had to give back the signing bonus. Mom feels that that was the start of all their problems with the IRS and somehow you're at fault because once you were emancipated you were no longer theirs to command. That put them in a very difficult position."

Roxanne sat down. That movie had been a cursed movie from the start. Even though the producers were able to get another actress, the movie was panned by critics and pretty much bombed at the box office. Her parents' contention had been that if she'd been the star the movie would have been perfect. Roxanne knew that wasn't the case—she'd read the script—but her parents were like a dog with a bone.

"Dad and Mom are in trouble with the IRS because they didn't report income." Even now, years later, Roxanne had no idea what her dad had done with the money and he'd never volunteered the information. "This is all on them and not my problem."

"They're making it your problem."

Roxanne felt a headache start at the back of her head. She knew they had no case but being embroiled in a legal battle was going to be a pain in the ass—and very public. And it would do exactly what she and the producers of *Celebrity Dance* didn't want: Roxanne overshadowing the other contestants in an unprecedented way.

Nick had finished his sandwich and water. "First off," he said quietly, "I know Trudy Mendoza is your lawyer and before you do anything else you need to speak to her."

"Good idea," Donna said. "We can't all get our panties in a knot when we don't have all the facts."

"I agree," Roxanne said. "Everybody have a cookie and then go home. I'm tired and I don't want to think about this until tomorrow."

Portia grabbed her and kissed her. She took two cookies and handed one to Tristan. "Come on. Let's get out of here."

Tristan watched Roxanne. He looked so lost, but she

couldn't help. She hugged and kissed him. "Everything will turn out all right."

"I'm sorry," he said suddenly and kissed her back. "I've done more than you know to keep this fight going. I…" He took a deep breath. "I've always been jealous of you. Everything comes so easy to you and Mom and Dad."

Roxanne put her finger over his mouth. "Hush. I've struggled with my own feelings. Mom and Dad always seemed to like you better than me. Hurt exists on both sides, but we're not going to rehash this. Not now. Not ever. You're my brother and I love you even if I don't always like your lifestyle or your decisions."

Portia hooked her arm through her brother's and pulled him toward the front door. She gave a last wave as she opened the door and left.

Roxanne handed a cookie to Nick. "Thank you for bringing me home."

"But you need me to go, too," he said, with a teasing smile.

"I do tonight." She walked him to the front door and gave him a long kiss. "I'll see you tomorrow at rehearsal."

Roxanne returned to the kitchen. Donna was cleaning up. She put plates in the dishwasher and washed the table.

"Don't worry," Donna said quietly. "This is nothing more than a five-year-old throwing a tantrum."

"Do you really think they can win something like this?"

"No. I'm wondering why they think they can intimidate you. Intimidation has never worked before."

"But they always had Tristan and Portia in the wings," Roxanne said.

"You're not going to give in."

Roxanne shook her head. "If my parents want a fight, I'm going to give them one."

The next day's rehearsal was a disaster. All the clumsy moves she thought she'd conquered came back and she finally sat on the ground trying not to cry.

Nick sat on the floor next to her and held her hand.

"I can't concentrate," she moaned.

"You're upset."

"This is crazy. I don't know why I'm obsessing over a nonsense suit that hasn't even been filed yet."

"Stop thinking about them. This is about this." Nick leaned over and kissed her deeply and thoroughly.

"It's working," she said, rubbing her forehead, trying to banish the headache throbbing behind her eyes. "I tossed and turned all night trying to think what I can do, but nothing came to me." What she wanted to do was move to Alaska.

"You can't do anything, except stop letting this situation bother you. Or at least don't let anyone who matters see how they bother you. You can talk to me."

She leaned against him. "The worry is throwing me off my game."

"Me, too." He ran a hand up and down her back and then turned her slightly as he began to knead at the knot of muscles down her spine.

She let him work on her back. His fingers poked and prodded, loosening the tension little by little.

"You have to hold your head high and not let people see how you're being affected by this. I don't know how the public is going to react, or how your parents are going to react, but you have to show you aren't being defeated by their actions." He kissed her. "Now, get up. Get your head together and learn the rumba."

"You're bossy today."

He kissed her. "You don't let me get away with that too often, so I'm owning my moment."

Roxanne laughed, pushed herself to her feet and held out her hands. "Let's get started."

Roxane's doorbell chimed. Nick looked up from the chart he'd been studying. Roxanne jumped off her chair and walked down the hall to answer the door. She already knew who was there since the guard at the gate had called her and she'd told him to let her parents' lawyer in.

"Ben Hardy," she said, "I figured you'd be showing up soon."

"Hello, Roxanne," he said. "May I come in?"

She stood aside to allow him to enter.

Benjamin Hardy had been her parents' lawyer for years. He was a short, round man with a receding hairline and somber brown eyes. He'd grown a beard since she'd last seen him and she had to admit it looked good on him.

He walked into the kitchen and set a briefcase down on the counter. "We have to talk."

"I figured. What do my parents want? Besides my soul."

He opened his briefcase after a brief glance at Nick. Nick smiled at him and made no move to leave.

"Stop being so dramatic, Roxanne."

"Me, dramatic!" She took a deep breath. "My parents have the market cornered for drama."

"Yes, but for them it's expected. From you, not so much." Ben pulled a manila file folder out of his briefcase.

"My parents aren't going to sue me." She spoke more confidently than she felt. "They don't have the money for a drawn-out court case that will air out all the dirty laundry and I know you don't work for free."

Ben frowned. "Be smart, Roxanne." He handed the folder to her. "If this goes to court, just getting the wrong judge can make a huge difference."

Roxanne didn't open the folder. She didn't want to know what was inside. "You came to see me. So what do you want to tell me?"

"Your parents are willing to drop the suit if you agree to encourage Portia and Tristan to renew their contracts and agree to star in the movie they are asking you to do."

Roxanne studied Ben. "Thank you for letting me know the terms of this offer. I need to think. You've had your say. I think it's time for you to leave."

Ben kept his cool. He smiled politely at Roxanne and Nick.

"Here," Roxanne said, "take one of Grandma's croissants. I know you love them." She packed one into a napkin and then led him back through the house and out the front door.

"Roxanne," Ben said, "you're playing with fire."

"Maybe. How do you think it's going to look when

the public finds out that my parents aren't loving and kind. What kind of parent sues their child? If you want to get nasty, I'll put my teary-eyed grandmother in front of the camera. She can sway the hardest of hearts."

Ben shook his head. "Roxanne..."

"I refuse to be blackmailed by my parents." She opened the front door and gestured for him to leave.

Ben descended the porch steps and walked down the sidewalk to his Mercedes parked at the curb. He turned one last time to look at Roxanne. She shook her head. He got in and drove away. She watched as he turned the corner before she returned to the kitchen.

Nick gave her a lingering kiss that sent her blood racing, despite her unease with the encounter with Ben.

"You have no idea how resentful I am right now," Roxanne said. "My parents have never been parents. From the second I did my very first commercial when I was four, they looked at me like I was an ATM. How do you deal with that?"

"I can tell you my parents tried to discourage me and my siblings from entering the business and with the exception of Nina and Matteus, who's a cop, we all ended up in it anyway."

"But you made the decision for yourself."

"I think if we would have quit at any time, my parents would have been happy. Show business is fickle."

She leaned into him. He slid his arms around her and held her tight. Just listening to him calmed her. "Not only that, show business is hard. I have the sore feet to show for it."

"For every Ann Miller who danced until the day she died, most of us are done by the time we're forty."

"Sometimes I feel like I never did enough for Portia and Tristan."

His arm tightened. "Whoa. In order to save others, you have to save yourself first. You put your oxygen mask on first before you put the mask on your child. You got out. You saved yourself first."

But the guilt just wouldn't go away. "Grandma saved me. She pointed out to me that if I emancipated myself, I wouldn't have to do anything I didn't want to do. She backed me up." She realized her grandmother had saved herself first, then Roxanne. Now Roxanne had to pay it forward. Donna had tried to help Portia and Tristan, but they hadn't been as close to their grandmother as Roxanne had been. And somehow, her parents had managed to keep Donna away.

He opened the front door and stepped out onto the porch. Shadows darkened the street as twilight approached. The heat was just as sizzling now as it had been earlier in the day.

He kissed her, his lips soft against hers. She almost wished he'd spend the night, but she and her grandmother needed some alone time.

"I'll see you in the morning at rehearsal," Nick promised.

She nodded and watched him walk to his car, get in and drive away just as Portia pulled into the driveway, got out of her car and slammed the door.

Portia followed Roxanne into the house, the air-conditioning humming in the background.

"I think we're in for a really hot summer," Donna said as she stirred a fresh-made pitcher of lemonade. Portia nibbled at a croissant, looking troubled.

"Then I'm moving to Alaska," Roxanne said. "That would put me out of most everyone's reach, because no one in this family would go."

Portia laughed. "I don't know about that. Mom and Dad are angry enough to hunt you down even if you moved to another galaxy."

"If they really want to get into producing, they could develop a whole series with parents feeling sorry for themselves because their children left them," Roxanne said.

"I'll suggest it to them." Portia rubbed her temples. "They could get a whole group of Hollywood parents in the same boat. They could do competitions, scavenger hunts or group therapy sessions. I ought to pitch it to them. Maybe then, they'd leave me alone for the rest of my life."

"Let's put everything on the back burner," Roxanne said. "Get a good night's sleep and we'll deal with this in the morning."

"Aren't you supposed to be learning to rumba?" Portia said.

"I am. I already ache from the twisting and turning and the constant reminders to smile and keep my chin up." Not to mention the fact she'd stepped on Nick's toes so many times in the past two days, even he complained.

"Let's take a long soak in the hot tub and then get some sleep." Portia gathered up her things. "I have to be at the zoo early tomorrow."

"And I'm working on a little something," Donna said, a mysterious look in her eyes.

"What?" Roxanne asked curiously.

Donna shrugged. "Still cooking. I'll let you know when it's done."

Roxanne didn't press her grandmother. Donna wasn't going to give up whatever she was working on until she was ready. Instead she sat down in the living room to look over the contents of the folder Ben had given her. Inside she found a contract for the movie and a copy of the lawsuit. Her parents seemed serious, but Roxanne wasn't playing their game.

Roxanne was able to secure an appointment with her lawyer for later in the day. She arrived at the rehearsal hall after a quick session with Fay to try on her costume for the next episode.

She found Nick already waiting for her, doing stretching exercises. He had a grim look on his face.

"Did you find out the information you wanted to find out?" Roxanne joined him in stretching, sitting on the floor and copying his moves.

"Your parents don't have a leg to stand on. They can't force you to tell them anything."

"That doesn't stop them from being nasty. I've been afraid to look at their social media pages. I'm sure they're ranting and raving over the injustice of a daughter who has no sense of appreciation for all their dedication, love and support. Blah. Blah. Blah. But I'm here to rumba, so let's dance." She pushed herself to her feet with her arms held out to him and smiled.

"Let's dance."

Chapter 11

Roxanne's lawyer had her office off Wilshire Boulevard in Santa Monica. The two-story brick-and-stucco building was set back from the street. They entered a courtyard with a circular fountain and headed toward the sliding glass door leading into the building. A discreet brass plaque on the side of a carved walnut door announced Mendoza and Mendoza, Attorneys at Law.

Trudy Mendoza was as beautiful now as she had been thirty years ago on the New York catwalk. Tall and still slim, her skin was a soft cinnamon and her eyes a light amber. Her black hair was threaded with gray and her face was aging gracefully without the benefit of plastic surgery.

"Welcome," Trudy said, her voice a deep contralto.

"Nick Torres. I haven't seen you in a long time. How's your mother?"

"She's good. Getting ready for her first grandchild and driving Nina nuts with all her plans for the nursery."

Trudy laughed.

"You two know each other," Roxanne said.

Trudy nodded. "I helped Grace and Manny, Nick's parents, out of a jam a number of years ago."

"I forget how small a world the Hollywood scene is," Roxanne said.

Trudy simply smiled. She sat down next to Roxanne. "So what's going on?"

Roxanne explained about her parents' threatening lawsuit. She showed her the lawsuit and the contract for the movie. Nick added a few details.

"They're attempting to do what?" Disbelief warred with astonishment on Trudy's face.

"Intimidate me and bring me back into the loving arms of my family," Roxanne replied, her tone sarcastic.

"Your parents are going to have a hard time proving you've interfered with their business or that you've influenced your siblings to leave their agency. And the burden of proof is on them. But I don't think you can ignore this. The scuttlebutt on the street says they've being losing clients."

"There's something else," Roxanne said quietly. "I've been thinking about this for a couple days. I want to make another offer to my parents. It might help them loosen their strings on Portia and Tristan, sweeten the deal and give me some leverage. I'm willing to pay my dad's IRS tax bill off in full."

She'd thought about it long and hard and as much as she hated to do it, she knew it would go a long way toward keeping the peace in her family—or at least for Portia and Tristan. They were stuck in the middle of her feud with her parents and the only way they could be free was if Roxanne took away the black cloud hanging over her parents.

Trudy nodded, surprise on her face. "You're a better daughter than they deserve. Let me do some research and we'll set up another meeting. I'll call you."

Roxanne survived the next two elimination rounds. She learned to rumba and to swing dance. She loved the swing dancing. Each routine became progressively harder. Nick was so patient with her.

"I'm a dancer." Roxanne sat on the floor of the dance studio putting on her sneakers. Rehearsals had become longer and more involved.

Nick laughed. "Yes, you are."

"Not a very good one," she said. "But I'm better than I used to be."

"Way better than you used to be." He sat on the floor next to her.

She leaned against him, his skin moist from exertion. If not for the anxiety of her parents' problems hanging over her head, she would have enjoyed the past two weeks more. Nick spent a lot of time at her house and having him around made her happy in a way she'd never been happy before. And having him in her bed made her even happier. The feel of his skin against her in the darkness of the night sent her heart pounding and heat spiraling through her. He also made her feel safe.

On the way out to her car, Trudy Mendoza called. Roxanne put the lawyer on speakerphone for Nick to hear, as well.

"Your parents rejected your offer," Trudy said. "They were quite forceful in their objections. But they did make a counteroffer. They're willing to let Portia and Tristan out of their contracts if you sign on to this movie they want you to do. Things have changed. They have a major star who is interested in the movie and it now looks like it's going be a theatrical release rather than a TV movie. Which means their financial percentage is going to increase a thousandfold."

Roxanne stopped in the middle of the parking lot uncertain whether to laugh or scream in frustration. "That's not going to happen."

"I agree," Nick said.

"Do you have a counteroffer?" Trudy asked.

"They can kiss my behind," Roxanne said, irritation in every syllable.

Trudy laughed. "I suggested they not be so hasty in turning down your generous offer and gave them a week to think about it. Though I'm pretty sure they are still going to turn you down."

"Of course they are," Roxanne said with a sigh. Her parents had been playing the game a long time. They wanted to transition to producing their own movies and TV shows. They still had a decent enough stable of actors in their agency to do that, despite the loss of so many. She just didn't like the way they were going about it.

Trudy said, "I don't have anything else to deal with."

"I thought I had enough leverage with the tax bill and that they'd jump at the idea of my paying it off. That would put them free and clear and give them a new start."

"From what I can tell, they aren't afraid of the IRS," Trudy said. "In fact, they don't seem to be afraid of anything."

"Let me think about this," Roxanne said. "I'll talk to my grandmother and see what she's thinking. Maybe she has some ideas." She disconnected and turned to Nick. "Well, you heard."

Nick nodded. "We'll come up with something."

Nick opened her car door just as her phone rang again.

"Grandma," Roxanne said, "is everything all right?"

"Get home quick and bring Nick with you." Donna hung up, leaving Roxanne with her mouth open in surprise. "You heard her. I'm to bring you home."

"I'll follow you."

Roxanne entered the kitchen to find her grandmother pacing back and forth.

"What's wrong? Did something happen to Tristan or Portia?" Roxanne grabbed her grandmother's hand.

"No, nothing like that. But before we go any further, you do have enough money to bail me out of jail, don't you?"

Roxanne frowned, dread filling her. "Did you do something?"

"No, but I'm about to." Donna led Roxanne and Nick back into the dining room. Her laptop was open and a few papers littered the tabletop. "I discovered something and for a moment I didn't know what I was looking at."

"You need to explain."

Donna put her hands on her hips. "I hired a private investigator."

"You did?" Roxanne stared at her grandmother in surprise.

"Of course I did. Two can play that game. I know more about being sneaky than my son and his wife will ever know." She handed a sheet of paper to Roxanne and then several photographs.

Roxanne glanced at the paper which appeared to be some sort of report. She handed it to Nick and then looked at the photos. "What am I looking at?"

"That is your father walking into the Saint Ann's Preparatory School in Anaheim Hills."

Roxanne was confused. The next photo showed her father coming out with two children, a boy and a girl. The girl looked to be seven, maybe eight years old and was cute with bouncy black hair and wearing a daisy costume. The boy was older, maybe ten or eleven, but his resemblance to the little girl told Roxanne they were siblings.

The next photo showed her father putting the children into his car.

"What is Dad doing with those two children?"

Donna handed Roxanne a close-up of the girl. "Doesn't she look familiar to you?"

"She looks like me at that age." Roxanne clutched the photo suddenly realizing what she was looking at. "Am I seeing what I think I'm seeing?"

Nick handed her the PI's report. "Read this."

She took the report and her mouth fell open in shock. "My father has another family?"

"Yes, he does," Donna said, pausing to let the information sink in. "But look at the bright side."

"There's a bright side!" Roxanne glanced through the photos a second time.

Donna handed her another photo of a striking Hispanic woman with long black hair that fell almost to her waist. She was tiny and so beautiful Roxanne could only stare at her. "My father has a mistress and I have half siblings."

"I have grandchildren I've never met." Donna tapped the photo with an agitated finger. "Do you know what this means?"

"My dad's a dead man."

"No. He's not a dead man, he's got a secret and we found out."

"I wonder if Mother knows," Roxanne said.

"I have no idea, but what do you think will happen when she finds out?"

Roxanne thought about her mother for a second and felt a second of sadness that her mother's world was about to fall apart. Even Roxanne felt betrayed. Her mother would feel that way many times greater.

She hugged her grandmother. "You're my hero." She regretted what she was about to do, but knew she'd still do it.

Nick looked at the photos. "I'm totally not surprised and surprised that I'm not surprised."

"He is his father's son," Donna said sadly. "If your grandfather were still alive, I'd be giving him a piece of my mind for being such a poor role model."

Roxanne knew her grandfather had left Donna for his mistress, but they'd never married and fortunately had no children.

"What should we do with this information?"

"Give it to Trudy." Nick placed the photos on the table. "This is your ace in the hole."

"If my mother doesn't know, I wouldn't want to be anywhere near her when she finds out." Roxanne picked up the photos and looked through them again analyzing her feelings. She wasn't surprised, either. She did feel sorry for those two children and her mother. She wondered if all the money she'd made during her years on *Family Tree*, which her father never explained what he did with, had something to do with this second family.

The woman's name was Carmen Lucero. The children were Yesenia and Dante. Roxanne wondered what the woman was like and why was she willing to take her father's leftovers.

"This is right up there with finding out I had a grandfather I didn't know about." Nick sighed.

"Welcome to our world." Roxanne gave him a kiss. "I told you secrets have a way of coming out."

"You weren't expecting this kind of a secret."

"Actually, I think in some way I knew my dad had a secret he was keeping from us. I'm sorry."

"Sorry about what?" Nick asked.

"My father's a jerk. I'm mad because he hurt my grandmother."

"I'm not hurt," Donna said.

"You should be."

Donna shook her head. "I stopped being hurt years ago. The only person responsible for this behavior is Eli. I wish I'd been smart enough to hire that detective earlier."

"We know now." Roxanne started to tremble. How could her family be so dysfunctional? Nick slid an arm around her, holding her close.

"How do you think Portia and Tristan will feel when they find out they have a half brother and sister?" Donna asked.

"Portia will be fine. She's going to love having a Mini-Me following her around, assuming our dad lets us meet them. I don't know about Tristan. He's always been the only boy and now he has competition." Roxanne peered at the photo of the boy. He looked more like Tristan than she'd thought. He had the same features, the same quirky smile. But when he looked at his father, he had a solemn look on his face.

"How do you feel?"

"I'm both happy and sad," Roxanne responded.

"Why happy and sad?" Nick's arm tightened around her.

"Because my dad is such a cliché. And I wonder where this secret is going to take us."

"We won't know until Trudy can take a look at the report and photos." Nick released Roxanne and gathered up the photos and report. "In fact, if I leave now

I can drop this off at her office before it closes for the day." He kissed Roxanne.

She wanted to cling to him, feeling overwhelmed. She saw him to the door and waved as he backed out of the driveway.

"Nick is turning into quite the knight in shining armor," Donna said.

Roxanne sighed wistfully. "I know."

"What do you intend to do about that?"

Roxanne simply shrugged.

Tension grew on the set. Another elimination round left Roxanne still in the competition. She was breathless with her success. She'd fulfilled her obligation to Nancy, uncovered her inner dancer and found Nick. Every time she glanced at him she felt a deep sense of admiration for him. He never complained, he never questioned her and every episode he did everything he could to build her confidence and make her look good. She loved being with him. She loved the feel of his arms around her. *All right, be honest*, she told herself. She loved him.

Nick made her feel as though she were truly a valued partner. And as her ratings went up, so did her confidence. Even Nancy had commented on how well Roxanne and Nick worked together.

He glanced at her as though he could feel her watching him. He strolled over and sat down next to her.

"Your mom is in the audience. I don't see your dad." Nick pointed at the monitor as the camera panned across the spectators.

"She makes me more nervous than my dad. Every time she criticizes me on TMZ, the comments hurt a little more. I didn't think I would feel hurt, but I do. No wonder my dad needs money with all the mouths he has to feed." She wondered how he'd react once the news of his second family got out. How would her mother act?

Nick chuckled. The show ended and Nick walked her out to her car only to find her mother's Range Rover parked next to it.

Her mother stalked toward her. "You know, Mom, being stalked in parking lots is getting old."

Her mother glared at her. "All you have to do is agree to do the movie. It's tailor-made for you."

"No." Roxanne looked around. "Where's Dad?"

Her mother shrugged. "Gone. He's gone a lot, trying to keep our current clients and find new ones," Hannah said angrily. "And you're not helping."

Roxanne's stomach roiled in tension. Why couldn't her parents love their children for what they were? She'd never get an answer to that question and didn't know why she kept asking it. Yet something inside her wanted their approval no matter how old she was.

"I have to get home." She sidestepped her mother. All the way to her car she could feel her mother's anger.

Nick gave her a kiss on the cheek. "I'll see you tomorrow."

"I know. Bright and early." She tried not to be disappointed he wasn't coming home with her.

"Actually, no. Meet me for lunch at Pablo's. One o'clock. My brothers and I are having lunch with our newly found grandfather."

"What about your sisters?"

"We wanted Nina and Lola to come, but Nina isn't traveling right now since she's due to have her baby in a few weeks and Lola is in Tokyo on a job."

She smiled at him. "Have you told your mom yet?"

"No. We wanted to talk to him first and find out all the whys."

"Don't gang up on him. I'm sure he had his reasons for what he did. I'll see you tomorrow then." She kissed him and waved as he headed toward his car.

Trudy called the next morning and told Roxanne she set a three o'clock meeting with her parents and asked her to be there. Roxanne called Nick and told him about the appointment. Instead of meeting at Pablo's for lunch, Roxanne asked him to come to the house after meeting with Lionel, and they could go to the meeting together.

When they walked into Trudy's office, the tension was so thick, Roxanne started to feel ill. Nick held her hand tightly.

Her mother sat stiffly at the end of the conference table. Her father looked worried. Portia stood at the window staring out at the garden and Donna brewed tea. Tristan paced back and forth. Finally he sat next to Portia, but looked as though he wanted to be anywhere but there.

Hannah gave Roxanne a haughty look. "I don't care what you're offering, we are not going to accept."

Trudy held up a hand. "Listen to us first." She opened a folder. "Roxanne made a very generous offer and I think you do need to accept it."

"No." Hannah gave her husband a sharp glance when he didn't say anything.

"You do know that your son and daughter want to do different things."

Hannah shrugged.

Trudy continued. "Roxanne has also agreed to pay the IRS the full sum of back taxes owed by you and your husband."

Hannah glared at Roxanne. "No."

Eli glanced at his daughter. Something in his face told Roxanne he was willing to accept her terms.

Trudy slid a paper with photos clipped to it toward Hannah. "I didn't really want to use this card without talking to you first, Eli, but circumstances have changed."

Hannah glanced at the photos and then at her husband. "What is this?"

Roxanne clutched Nick's hand. The fireworks were about to start.

Trudy smiled. "It seems your husband has a secret."

Hannah's lips grew pinched and her eyes narrowed. She shoved the photos back at Trudy. "I already know this tawdry little secret."

"But," Trudy said, "do you want the world to know this tawdry little secret?"

"Blackmail is not going to work on me."

"I will do whatever it takes to get Portia and Tristan free of you," Roxanne said.

Hannah glared at Eli. He looked away, a guilty look in his eyes.

"We have a marriage in name only. You want to

blame everything on Roxanne, when really it's you and me. We've been falling apart for years," Eli stated quietly. "Accept the terms."

Roxanne braced for the storm.

"Accept the terms, Hannah." Eli's voice held a firmness Roxanne had never heard before. "I want it done. Trying to keep Roxanne on a short leash didn't work. Why would you think it's working with Tristan and Portia? They want out. Let them go," Eli said.

Roxanne said, "Portia and Tristan are unhappy and you don't look happy, either. You're a smart woman. You want to move into producing. I think you and Dad would be good at it. You have the talent already, you just need the right vehicle."

Eli tapped the table. "Hannah, we could find ten actresses in a minute who could do this movie you want Roxanne to do and be just as good at it. Let's find them."

Hannah screamed at Roxanne, "This is all your fault. You left us high and dry. From the day you signed your emancipation, you walked away and never looked back. You never once thought about how we felt."

"You wanted me to be in the equivalent of a soft-core porno movie. I was sixteen and didn't want to have anything to do with that film." Roxanne's voice rose as anxiety flooded her.

"It was a smart move." Hannah pounded the table with her fist, her voice was tinged with scorn. "You would have been established as an adult star."

"Calm down, Hannah," Eli said.

"Leah St. John," Roxanne said, "who accepted the role after I turned it down, committed suicide. She couldn't survive the critical nastiness. And the movie was so bad, even the studio was embarrassed."

"With you in the role, it would have been a success," Hannah said. Suddenly she fell back in her chair and took a deep breath as though rethinking her position.

"I was tired of being your puppet." Roxanne's voice rose despite her attempt to stay calm.

"Hannah," Eli said, strain starting to show in his features. "Leave Roxanne alone."

Hannah glared at her husband. "And if I don't?"

"I'm out. Our children hate us. I hate us. What have we turned into?"

"Obviously you turned into something else, into someone else," Hannah said nastily as she pounded the photo of his other family with a finger. "You betrayed me, have done so for years."

"We live from paycheck to paycheck. Our home is mortgaged to the hilt. You wanted a dynasty and instead we have sawdust in our shoes."

Hannah scoffed. "Is that your excuse for dallying with another woman?"

Eli sighed. "I've never stopped loving you. I just needed a vacation from the intensity. We could argue in divorce court for the next two years. Let Portia and Tristan go. You can start over."

Hannah slumped, defeat in her eyes. "Go back to your mistress. I can take care of myself." She glared at Trudy. "All right, we'll drop the lawsuit."

Trudy handed them a folder asking them to sign an official agreement. Her mother stabbed the pen at the paper as she angrily added her signature. She shoved the folder at Eli, stood and stalked from the room.

Roxanne didn't realize she was holding her breath until her mother was gone.

"I'm sorry, Roxanne, Portia," Eli said sadly. "Portia, I know you want to go to school. I wish you luck, Tristan. I think you're right, you belong on Broadway." He took a deep breath, stood and left the room.

Roxanne was stunned. "I was not expecting them to yield like this." She'd expected a war of epic proportions and felt a bit deflated. Though she had the feeling that no matter what, her mother would land on her feet.

Portia stared at her. "We're all free!"

Roxanne felt drained. She nodded, indicating the court reporter who sat so still and silently in the corner of the room trying to remain unnoticed. "It's all documented."

Roxanne's investments would take a minor hit, but as her new business grew, she'd be fine.

Portia looked tense. "I thought I'd be happier." She started to cry.

Tristan hugged her. "I know. I feel the same way."

Roxanne simply felt tired. She wanted to go home and hide. She turned to Nick and he put his arms around her, as though he knew exactly how she felt.

"Let's go home," Donna said. "Portia and Tristan, you come, too."

Chapter 12

Nick escorted Roxanne into the restaurant. He felt nervous trying to figure out how to talk to his mother about her father.

"Are you sure you want to present this information in this manner?" Roxanne asked in the reception area.

"Trust me, my mother is the kind who just rips the bandage off and gets to the source."

For midweek, the restaurant was busy. Roxanne looked around curiously.

"This way," Nick said gesturing toward the back of the restaurant to an area that was closed off from the main dining area by a half wall filled with potted plants.

His brothers had already arrived. Daniel grinned and waved at Nick. Next to him sat his fiancée, Greer. Nick's mother stood at the sideboard checking the food and talking to a waitress who nodded and turned to head back toward the kitchen. Matteus sat in a corner facing the room, his cop senses on alert as always. Sebastian held a deck of cards and was showing their father, Manny, his newest sleight of hand trick. Rafael, the youngest brother in the family, had called to cancel, citing a problem with one of his clients.

Grace looked up at Nick's arrival, her glance pausing a moment on Roxanne. A smile appeared on her face and she glided to Nick, gave him a kiss on the cheek and directed him to the end of the table with two plates.

"So," Grace said, "tell me what this meeting is all about." Again her gaze lingered on Roxanne who set her briefcase against her leg.

All eyes turned expectantly toward Nick.

"You know Roxanne Deveraux."

Grace nodded politely. "Roxanne, how nice to see you again."

"I had this idea…" Nick swallowed nervously. "I planned a family genealogy to give as Christmas gifts to everyone and asked Roxanne to do it."

"How interesting," Grace said her face alighted with curiosity. "I've always been curious about my family."

Nick looked at Roxanne and she smiled at him, opened her briefcase and brought out her charts.

"One of the side issues of a genealogical search is that family secrets stop being secrets." Roxanne opened the folder. "And before I go on—" she glanced at Nick nervously "—one item is rather sensitive. I wanted to excuse myself, but Nick…"

"Roxanne has all the answers," Nick said.

Grace's eyebrows rose. "I see," she said cautiously. "How sensitive is this, and is this going to make me cry?"

Roxanne didn't know what to say.

"I don't think you'll cry, but I wanted to do this more privately," Nick said, "but the right time never seemed to come around."

Grace patted Nick's face. "Whatever secret that has you in knots, I can take it. Nick, do you trust Roxanne?"

"I do," he said.

Grace nodded. "You've put a lot of work into this. Why don't you start and we'll see how it goes."

Roxanne laid the charts out in order. "We're going to work our way from the earliest evidence of your family I found to the present."

"This is exciting." Grace sat down looking expectant.

Roxanne handed her a drawing. "This is a drawing of your ancestor, Yasmin Portrero."

"She's beautiful," Grace said.

"She was the daughter of a man who was originally a sailor on a Spanish ship captured by English privateers, brought to England, assimilated into English society and eventually became a merchant. I haven't been able to locate his full name, but Yasmin appears to have been his only child and she's unique in that she married Sir John Wickes, a captain of the guard to Queen Elizabeth." Roxanne handed Grace a copy of the marriage vows listed in a church document.

"I come from English nobility?" Grace looked excited. "How far away am I from inheriting the throne of England?"

Nick laughed. Just like his mother to pick up on the obvious.

"Thousands will have to die," Roxanne said with a chuckle. "Yasmin and Sir John Wickes had several children and lived at Hampton Court. I don't know if she had any official position in the court, but I do know she is listed as a seamstress for the queen."

"They're black people, living next door to the queen. Was she a slave?"

"Most blacks during Elizabeth's time were captured sailors from Spanish ships. There's no record that Yasmin or her father were slaves. Some sailors returned to Spain, but many others stayed. At one time Queen Elizabeth felt that all the blacks—or blackamoors, as she called them—should be sent back to Spain because of their ties to Catholicism. But Yasmin's father most likely converted to the Church of England which is why he stayed." Roxanne shuffled through her charts.

"I didn't know there were blacks in England at this time."

"The first blacks showed up around 1550 and created a thriving community in London. Some were merchants, some were soldiers and some were servants." Roxanne glanced at Nick. "Don't get me wrong, life was hard for them and they did suffer, but then most of England suffered. Bathing was practically unknown and hygiene was minimal at best. And while dentists did exist, they mostly just pulled teeth."

"Wow," Grace said as she glanced through the charts and documents Roxanne had given her. "How did my ancestors get here?"

Roxanne gave her another document. "We have a gap in information. While I could find the names of Yasmin's and Sir John's descendants, no information about them appears to exist until a Dr. Charles Stanton immigrated to Philadelphia from London where he opened a medical school for black students."

"I know I was born in Philadelphia, and grew up in Atlanta. I also know my birth name was Grace Stanton."

"That brings us to the other interesting fact about your family tree." Roxanne handed her a copy of a marriage license. She glanced at Nick and he nodded for her to go on.

"If you're worried, I already knew that Al wasn't my biological father." Grace glanced through the next set of documents. "My mother told me my biological father died when I was a baby."

"This is where the sensitive information comes in," Roxanne said nervously. "I'll excuse myself and let Nick tell you."

Grace studied Roxanne. "You already know this and I'm sure you've dealt with sensitive issues before. I think you should stay. After all, you did all the work."

Roxanne glanced at Nick. His turn had come. "Mom." He took a deep breath. "Your father, Lionel Stanton, is still alive and he lives in Pasadena."

Grace looked shocked. She shook her head. "You're kidding me." She glanced back and forth between Roxanne and Nick.

Nick shook his head. This was harder than he thought it would be. "Not kidding you, Mom. I met him…"

"You met him…"

"I wanted to tell you first. I felt I owed you, but I ended up telling Sebastian and Daniel and we decided… Well, it just sort of happened and I ended up taking everyone but Nina and Lola to meet him yesterday."

Grace looked confused. "My mother told me he died."

"Here are the divorce papers." Roxanne slid a folder toward Grace.

Grace read through the papers. "This can't be right." She looked sad and vulnerable. Nick didn't know how to comfort her.

"I'm afraid it is," Roxanne said gently.

"Why would my mother lie to me?" Grace's voice trembled.

"I don't know, Mom," Nick replied. She couldn't even ask since her mother had passed away several years ago. "I called Grandpa Al and asked him, but he said your mom never said a word about Lionel and he never asked."

"I don't know what to say." Tears slid down her cheeks. Manny put an arm around Grace and held her tightly.

"He wants to meet with you," Nick said.

"Did he tell you why?" Grace clutched Manny's hand and wiped her tears.

Nick shook his head. "He said he would only tell you. Are you okay?"

Grace pressed her fingers to her eyes. "I have a lot to think about."

"You don't have to meet with him," Manny said.

"Of course I do. He's my father. What about Lola and Nina?"

"They both know. We had to talk Nina out of waddling herself down here. Lola said she'd be home on Sunday."

Grace was silent for several moments. "Set up a meeting."

Nick nodded at Roxanne. She reached down into her briefcase and pulled out a scrapbook. She handed the book to Nick and he handed it to his mother.

"Lionel gave me this," Nick explained. "He wanted you to see it."

Grace opened the scrapbook, her face taking on a look of wonder. Nick had been astonished when he'd first viewed the scrapbook. Inside was every news story, every review and every bit of information Lionel had been able to find about Grace.

Tears formed in Grace's eyes. She stood, clutched the scrapbook to her chest and left, walking swiftly through the dining room toward her office. Manny stood and started to follow his wife.

"Dad," Nick said. He hated seeing his mother hurt like this.

"Stay. Eat your dinner. I'll deal with your mother. Everything will be fine." Manny made his way across the dining room in Grace's wake.

"Wow," Daniel said. "I'm not sure how I expected that to go."

"It went better than I thought it would," Nick responded.

Roxanne gathered up all the documents and put them back in her briefcase. "I told you. Secrets have a way of coming out."

"Do you think she's mad at us?" Sebastian asked.

"She needs to process. This is big news." Nick turned to Roxanne. "Do these things happen to you all the time?"

"Without giving any names, a religious leader discovered that his great-grandmother was a madam, a bootlegger and a prominent crime figure in New Jersey during Prohibition."

Matteus laughed. "I'll bet that was a surprise."

"And then there were the assorted cousins who married cousins," Roxanne continued, "and in my own family, a black widow who spent her life murdering her husbands. You never know where something will lead."

"At least we have some nobility in our background."

"Minor nobility," Roxanne said.

"Let's eat," Nick said. "I think cocktails are in order."

"Lots of cocktails," Daniel said.

"Thank you for your support tonight," Nick told Roxanne as she unlocked the kitchen door. Portia and Donna were out and they would have the house to themselves.

"I'm sorry your mother was upset, but I think she's going to see this as a chance for something new and exciting."

"You did warn me. My mother is always optimistic."

She stepped into the kitchen, turning on the overhead light. "At least I got a terrific meal."

"You did." Nick held her tight, his breath warm on her cheek. "I need some alone time with you."

"You got it." She smiled as she led him up the stairs to her bedroom.

* * *

Alone time with Nick became more rare as the dance competition really started to heat up. Roxanne's life became more rehearsal, longer and more complicated routines and exhausted muscles.

She sat on the floor while Nick massaged the cramp from her calf.

"Tonight is the big night." She was amazed she'd lasted to the end.

"In more ways than one," Nick said.

"What does that mean?"

"*Celebrity Dance* has been renewed for two more seasons."

Roxanne sat stunned. "Really?"

"You'll never be a great dancer, but the audience loves you. And tonight you and I have a real shot at winning the trophy. And Mike wants you to come back for the next season as a celebrity judge."

She scoffed. "I don't know. I'll have to think about it." She already had several new clients and she wanted to get back to her business. She didn't know how much time she would have to commit to the show, but then again she'd just done ten weeks of intense rehearsal and still kept her business on track. She could probably handle being a judge easily enough.

He leaned in and kissed her. "You know a whole lot more than you think you do."

"The audience will think I'm there because I'm sleeping with you." She circled her arms around his neck and closed her eyes. He'd come to mean so much more than just a dance partner and business associate. Every moment spent with Nick left her wanting more.

He kissed her again, a long lingering kiss. "We are sleeping together." He paused, thinking. "What would happen if we were married to each other?"

"Is that a proposal?" Was he really proposing to her? Her heart raced with excitement.

"Yes. I love you," he said.

She leaned into him. "I love you, too." Something inside her blossomed and grew.

"That 'I love you' was a bit tentative." He sat back on his heels.

"I have no idea how to make a marriage work. The only model I have is my parents." And what a disaster that was.

"On what not to do," Nick said. "If you think your parents would do something, then don't do it. And my parents are great role models. If I do something stupid and you ask my mom and dad about it, they won't cut me any slack. They'll give you an honest answer and me a swift kick. So what's your answer."

"Yes, I'll marry you."

He hugged her. "Okay. Back to rehearsal."

Roxanne groaned.

Roxanne watched the monitors. Her parents were in the audience, along with Portia, Tristan and Donna. Even her father's mistress, Carmen, and her two children decided to attend. Portia said her mother had presented some sort of funky idea of being one big family to them and Carmen was apparently interested.

Roxanne hoped the two children weren't going to be involved.

Her heart fluttered nervously. Tonight's dance was the tango and she'd practiced and practiced the complicated dance routine wanting to excel at it.

Her costume was a slinky teal-and-green dress with fringe that hugged every curve on her body and showed more skin than she was usually comfortable with. The stylist had arranged her hair into a complicated tangle of curls with a mass of feathers embedded in the curls.

"Breathe," Nick said.

"But…"

"Just breathe and don't think about the other dancers."

They were last and each moment added to her anxiety.

"Are you ready to win this?" Nick tugged her hand.

She caressed his cheek. "I already did win. I won you."

The orchestra cued their music and Roxanne had one last moment to breathe before being pulled to the dance floor. The audience erupted into loud applause and whistles.

Roxanne stiffened into her pose. *Smile*, she told herself. *Keep your shoulders straight. You can do this.* Nick grasped her around the waist as the orchestra launched into the opening bars of Marc Anthony's "I Need to Know."

Roxanne whirled and dipped and moved with the sinuous flare that made the tango so sensual. When the routine ended, she stood breathlessly waiting for the judges to decide the final score. The moments ticked by. The other two dance teams were brought out and they stood in a line, waiting.

"Roxanne," one of the judges said. "You finally got it, my dear. Your dance was superb. Perfect."

"Yes. Perfect," echoed the second judge.

The three judges conferred for a moment and then held up three perfect scores.

"You won," Nick said.

Roxanne thought about fainting, but the excitement kept her on her feet.

Nancy came out with the trophy and handed it to Roxanne. "I knew you could do it." She kissed Roxanne and stepped back, turning to the camera. "Isn't she amazing?"

The audience broke into wild applause. Roxanne clutched the trophy with one hand and Nick's hand with the other. "Thank you."

"And thank you," Nancy said.

Nick drove to his parents' restaurant. Roxanne was still in shock. A bubbly kind of shock. She'd won. She even got to keep her trophy.

"We have a lot to celebrate," Nick told her.

"Are you going to tell your family about our engagement?"

"My mom knows everything about everything before we ever think it. Of course, I was supposed to pop the question after our great victory, not before."

Roxanne laughed. "They're not going to be disappointed, are they?"

"I doubt it. My parents don't care how I get married, they just worry about the who, and they really like you."

He pulled up to the restaurant ablaze with light and handed his car keys to the valet.

Inside was a blast of music, laughing and tantalizing food smells. Celebrations with his family were boisterous and chaotic. Tristan and Portia hugged Roxanne tightly, and her father stood in the background with his arm around his mistress. Their children stood with them, the little girl looking anxious and the boy looking defiant. And while meeting the whole Torres clan, minus the pregnant Nina, was overwhelming, Roxanne felt that she belonged.

"What a triumph for both of you. A trophy and a proposal all in one day." Grace handed flutes of champagne to Nick and Roxanne.

Nick gave Roxanne a knowing look. "I told you."

"Welcome to the family, Roxanne." Grace pushed her into the family area and started introducing her as the next daughter-in-law.

Nick hung back watching the woman he loved with his mother. Her sister hugged her and her brother gave her a huge kiss.

Donna grinned at her. "I'm happy for you."

Lionel Stanton stepped forward to shake hands with Roxanne. Nick could see that Lionel looked a little uncomfortable, but he was happy to see him.

Lionel leaned toward Nick. "Your mother and I made our peace."

"I'm glad."

"Don't let the woman you love get away because of your pride." Lionel stepped away.

His brothers pounded him on the shoulder and back. Lola kissed him and wished him well. Everyone sat at the tables. Grace tapped a glass and called for attention. Silence fell.

"To the newest addition to the Torres family," Grace announced. "Welcome."

Nick held Roxanne's hand. She smiled almost shyly. "You realize life is going to be crazy from here on."

"I do."

"I have an idea." She held up her hand for Grace's attention. "Thank you for the warm welcome, but Nick and I are going to be crazy busy and planning a wedding is going to take a lot of time."

"What's your idea?" Grace asked.

Roxanne turned to Nick. "Let's go to Vegas. Right now. Tonight and just get married. No muss, no fuss. Then we can get on with the business of living and loving."

"I like the way you think, future Mrs. Torres." Admiration filled him. He glanced at his mother, who smiled.

"I like the way she thinks, too." Grace glanced around. "We're all in."

"My show can do without me for a couple days," Daniel said with a wicked grin at Greer.

Greer shook her head. "Our wedding is already planned. I spent weeks designing the Rose Parade float we'll be married on and the minister has confirmed and the reception hall is booked. I want the world to know he's married to me. There is no going off to Las Vegas for a quickie wedding for us."

Nick saw the excitement in Roxanne's eyes. "Let's do this. Do you think your grandmother will mind?"

Roxanne glanced at her grandmother. Donna nodded slightly and glanced at Portia.

"She's good," Roxanne said. "Portia has always wanted a more traditional wedding."

Grace stood up. "Everyone eat first. I'll make a few calls and we can leave after dinner."

"Everyone?" Roxanne asked in surprise.

"I'm not letting my boy get married without the rest of us." She looked around, counting. "I figure six, maybe seven limos should do it. And we're not telling Nina until afterward or she'll be annoyed." She threaded her way around the tables and into the main dining room, her phone to her ear. "I'll be back in a few minutes."

"Are you sure you don't want all the bells and whistles and the big fancy wedding?" Nick asked.

"I'm sure. I just want to get on with the business of loving you and being married to you."

* * * * *

SPECIAL EXCERPT FROM

An ambitious daughter of a close-knit Louisiana clan, Kamaya Boudreaux is making a name for herself in the business world. But when her secret venture is threatened to be exposed, she needs to do some serious damage control. Her plans don't include giving in to temptation with her sexy business partner, Wesley Walters...

Read on for a sneak peek at A PLEASING TEMPTATION, the next exciting installment in author Deborah Fletcher Mello's ***THE BOUDREAUX FAMILY*** *series!*

Wesley reached into the briefcase that rested beside his chair leg. He passed her the folder of documents. "They're all signed," he said as he extended his hand to shake hers. "I look forward to working with you, Kamaya Boudreaux."

She slid her palm against his, the warmth of his touch heating her spirit. "Same here, Wesley Walters. I imagine we're going to make a formidable team."

"Team! I like that."

"You should. Because it's so out of character for me! I don't usually play well with others."

He chuckled. "Then I'm glad you chose me to play with first."

KPEXP0317

A cup of coffee and a few questions kept Kamaya and Wesley talking for almost three hours. After sharing more than either had planned, they stood, saying their goodbyes and making plans to see each other again.

"I would really love to take you to dinner," Wesley said as he walked Kamaya to her car.

"Are you asking me out on a date, Wesley Walters?"

He grinned. "I am. With one condition."

"What's that?"

"We don't talk business. I get the impression that's not an easy thing for you to do. So will you accept the challenge?"

As they reached her car, she smiled as she nodded her head. "I'd love to."

"I mean it about not talking business."

Kamaya laughed. "You really don't know me."

He laughed with her. "I don't, but I definitely look forward to changing that."

Wesley opened the door of her vehicle. The air between them was thick and heavy, carnal energy sweeping from one to the other, fervent with desire. It was intense and unexpected, and left them both feeling a little awkward and definitely excited about what might come.

"Drive safely, Kamaya," he whispered softly, watching as she slid into the driver's seat.

She nodded. "You, too, Wesley. Have a really good night."

Don't miss A PLEASING TEMPTATION
by Deborah Fletcher Mello, available April 2017
wherever Harlequin® Kimani Romance™
books and ebooks are sold.

KPEXP0317